Madam President

O. L. Gregory

ISBN: **1508550417**
ISBN-13: **978-1508550419**

CONTENTS

PROLOGUE

Something was up.

My gaze had left the teleprompter to make eye contact with the audience. As I scanned around, my eyes came to land on a Secret Service agent in the back of the room who put a finger on his earpiece, to shove it in a little deeper, in order to hear a little better. I kept on talking, kept on scanning. And then I saw another agent to my left do the same thing as the other agent had.

My eyes went to George, who was standing guard by the main door. He lifted his arm to speak into the small microphone hiding under his sleeve. No look of impending doom, no hard set of the mouth, nothing was showing on his face. So, I kept on talking and put my eyes back on the teleprompter to pick up my next talking point.

Then the two agents waiting in the wings of the stage moved in to flank me.

I just kept talking, having been taught to ignore the ripple of flutters that sometimes went through the team. Whatever it was, they'd take care of it. The less attention I paid to it, the less likely that my audience would be bothered by it. The last thing we needed was to cause a panic while the team checked out something that almost always turned out to be nothing.

I was on to my next point when the agent to my right cleared his throat. I turned my head just enough to catch him in my peripheral vision and he gave me a single, small nod.

My mouth went dry.

George and his number two man moved forward from the doorway. They began walking up the center aisle, straight for me...

1

1 GUILTY PLEASURES

Technically, I had no right to wake up within the walls of the White House. But that hadn't stopped Dad from offering to have me live here, or me from accepting. We were the only family either of us had left. It didn't take a genius to figure out why we liked to keep the other one close.

When Dad first told me that he was going to run for President, I laughed. I figured he didn't have a chance. No one even really knew him. He was a blue-collar worker, for crying out loud.

Then the campaign started, people heard him speak, he answered their questions, and that had been the beginning of the end. His numbers shot up week after week. Next thing I knew, I was asked to step in and help him campaign because he no longer had a wife. I took a leave of absence from my job, fully intending to return to it after the election.

It started looking more and more as if he had a shot at winning. It was at that point Dad asked me what my plans were, if he won. I told him that I figured on going back to my life. I'd keep on living in the house, without him, and I'd go back to my job. I figured my life would more or less go back to the way it was. Yeah, the windows would be bulletproof, and they might stick a security guy or two around me, but my life would pretty much go back to normal.

That had been my plan. Dad's plan looked a little different.

First, they offered for me to substitute in the traditional role of First Lady. They said I could fill that office, pick a cause, and have at it.

I didn't like that plan. Too much smiling, nodding, handshaking, and pleasantries. I was full of sass and vinegar; I'd never be able to pull it off.

Then one night, over a couple of Long Island iced teas, Dad offered me the office of Vice President.

I laughed in his face.

The next night, he started having other people on the campaign start making comments about how I should run. I tracked Dad down and told him to make it stop.

The next morning, he sent me a singing telegram, inviting me to join the campaign. I tipped the guy fifty bucks to go sing a song of jubilant denial to my father.

That afternoon, someone leaked my running to the press. I spent the evening dodging interviews.

The following day, he spent every extra second he had sending me a barrage of texts, all but begging me to put my name on the ticket. I ignored the first thirty. I started plotting against him after the fortieth message. After the fiftieth, I sent him a picture of a call girl and threatened to send her to his hotel room that night and film her approaching his door and knocking in a pretend code and then sending the footage to the local news stations.

He stopped texting after that. But the next morning, he was participating in an interview on a television show and I was in the wings, watching. They invited me to come on stage. I was preparing to give my standard set of answers as to why I supported my father's unheard-of campaign as I approached the couch to sit.

But before I could get started, Daddy decided to corner his little girl. He smiled and started listing the issues upon which we agreed. Then he told me that if I wanted to stop complaining about our education system and actually try to do something about it, I'd have his backing to pursue it. Or I could go on home, return to teaching within the current system, and trust somebody else to try and fix it.

I didn't want to say yes, but I couldn't seem to say no.

I agreed to run, I put my name on the ticket, and we won. And now, every morning my alarm goes off at three a.m. And every morning I hit the ten-minute snooze button three times. At three-thirty, I drag myself out of bed, still half asleep.

Even though the house has a fully loaded gym in the basement, my bear-like tendencies first thing in the morning keep me far from being social. So, the staff brought a treadmill into my room and set it up shortly after Dad and I moved in.

In the dark, I feel my way over to the treadmill, hit a button, and begin my daily workout. I keep one hand on the bar, so I don't fall off the thing, and reach out to the mini-fridge on the table next to me with the other hand to grab a bottle of water. This is how I like my mornings, with only the glow of the lights on the treadmill's dash, and in as much silence as the machine will allow. I get my blood flowing, start hydrating, and wonder exactly what it would take to convince this government to become nocturnal.

By four, I'm in the tub. I climb in with my e-reader and pick a novel to read for pure pleasure. I keep low lighting on in the bathroom, trying to get my brain to adjust to the idea of being up for the day. I unwrap the piece of chocolate housekeeping leaves by the tub for me every morning, put it in my mouth, and let it melt on my tongue. My 'me' time is about done and the chocolate takes the sting out of that knowledge.

By five, I'm back in the room where someone has laid out an appropriate outfit for the day's schedule and there's now hot tea waiting for me. They know I like my tea strong, so they dump bags straight into the thermal cup of water to steep and leave them in there.

I get dressed, spray my hair, swipe on a little makeup, slip on some heels, and drink half my carafe of tea to fortify myself for the nonstop day ahead.

I force myself to get up and take the time to do this every morning because I know that once I leave my bedroom, the day is no longer mine. Too many days without any time for myself, and I begin to forget who I am under the business suit.

Five-thirty comes and I'm downstairs, in my office, and sitting behind my desk with a plate of fresh fruit. The news is on, I'm looking over my schedule, and I'm wondering why in the hell I ever let my father talk me into taking this job.

Oh, yeah, now I remember. He doesn't trust anyone else to continue his agenda if something should happen to him. There's no one else in DC like him and he doesn't want everything he's spent the past few years working on to go down the drain if he keels over with a heart attack or something.

I shook my head at the thought, *the things I do for my father.*

Will, the Deputy Chief of Staff, comes in first thing every morning to touch-base with me. He was the guy who kept communications between my father's office and my office going. Dad and I talked about what we were doing, but Will kept up on the day-to-day progress.

Will was a smart man, who never tried to contact me in the wee early morning hours. He understood that while I might be conscious, I had a peaceful morning routine, that kept me sane, to adhere to. Six o'clock rolls around and he comes in, says "Good morning" on his way from the door to me, and steals a kiss or two or three, knowing that right now is the most relaxed I'm going to be all day.

There's not much of a chance for a dating life with this job. Even if I did have the time, there was no way I was going to date in the public eye. There's not a single person in existence that somebody out in the public wouldn't crucify me for being seen with.

The kind of easy-going relationship that Will and I have works for us. Touching-base in the morning, a shared lunch here and there, and private 'meetings' upstairs at the end of a sixteen-hour day is all that keeps an 'us' going.

With our time being so limited, little flirtations went a long way between us. Sometimes, when I had papers for my secretary to send over to his office, I'd put a sticky note under the top page with a heart drawn on it. And other times, he'd bring me in a flower from the rose garden that I was supposed to think he'd snuck out and picked himself, when really he'd gotten a gardener to do it so they wouldn't yell at him for stealing it.

No, I don't think there's much of a future for the two of us. There's not even time for a chance for us to try to build towards a future. But what we did have is now, and for now, I sure did enjoy passing stolen moments of time with him. The thing was that we'd been together for so long, feelings were starting to run a little deep, and it was getting harder and harder to keep it light and easy between us.

Dad was always in his office by six. And by that hour of the day, the morning man had already swum laps, showered, dressed, eaten breakfast, watched the news, bantered back and forth with the Secret Service over sports scores from the night before, asked about people's kids, and was briefed over happenings in the building overnight. By six-thirty, I was in the oval, by his side, and we were going over things for the day.

I'm not the typical vice president. I'm not kept on the sidelines and only trotted out when someone needed something. I actually work in a partnership with the President. I did have my pet projects, but Dad and I saw eye to eye on them. And when we didn't, we still understood and appreciated the other's point of view, and Dad would assign someone else, if possible. Otherwise, we used my job, and our agreeing viewpoints, to our advantage.

Senior staff met at seven. Sometimes I stayed, and sometimes I was excused. Then a hug for Dad, because he was my Dad, and on with whatever mess the day held in store for me.

By eight o'clock, on this particular morning, our personal secretaries were tag-teaming Dad and me. With the next state dinner coming up, would the President and Vice President be escorting each other again?

Dad and I escorting each other solved a few problems. It saved Dad from having to go stag and letting it look like the most eligible bachelor in the world couldn't manage to get a date. It also spared him from having to find a date that could deal with that kind of pressure, and the month's worth of fallout he'd be slammed with for his choice in dates, no matter who she was.

In turn, it saved me from making my relationship with the Deputy Chief of Staff public knowledge. It also spared me the other option of having to go stag and then having the adult children of the other heads of state hit on me, with pictures and public opinions published the next day about whom I'd danced with.

Being hit on by a European prince may sound like an awesome way to pass a boring, politics filled evening, but it's really not. Most princes aren't *the* prince of their respective country. — The fantasy of a princely romance gets shattered once you realize the throne isn't in their future. — And Prince Charming never had any annoying idiosyncrasies that drove Cinderella insane like these guys did. And then there are the cultural differences that get in the way, if you could get past some of their political views.

That's not even taking into consideration that you'd then be trying to carry on some form of a relationship from two different continents. No, thank you. I couldn't carry on a proper relationship from inside the same building. Besides, I was willing to bet that I did more in a day to serve my country than the vast majority of them did to serve theirs in a year. Most princes, children of prime ministers, or kids of other presidents didn't impress me.

Many times, if they had a title, it merely meant that they were related to someone who did the actual work for their country. I had a title to show that I worked for the country I represented at these affairs. I got my hands dirty before I put on the evening gown.

Do you know what the job of the Vice President actually is? I am the president of the US Senate. Granted, that sounds a lot fancier and more prestigious than it is. At times, it feels like a babysitting job, and I do have the option to appoint someone else to do it, if it gets too annoying.

But, I hold a unique position between two branches of government. Some people argue that I'm part of the executive branch, because I'm next in line for our version of the throne and because I work out of the White House, in conjunction with the President. Some say I'm part of the legislative branch because I preside over the Senate. There have been actual debates about it, sometimes by scholars and historians, sometimes by budget writers who'd rather the other branch pay for the position. The real kicker in the debate is that the Constitution doesn't make it clear.

I take all of that to mean that I hold the position of one of those checks and balances built into the system to make sure no one branch becomes more powerful than another. Personally, that's why I think that, throughout the history of our government, both sides have tried to make the role of the Vice President smaller and smaller. They're trying to keep the other branches out of their business.

Dad and I don't see it that way. He doesn't treat me as a mere substitute on standby. I'm in on his plans. And I rarely leave the President Pro-Tempore of the Senate, the number two man over there, to oversee the day-to-day proceedings of the Senate without me. I keep my hands in on both sides. And why? Because I actually want to see that something gets done, instead of both sides just talking and fighting about it.

I've been known to lecture about not posturing, stalling, and arguing about every little thing. I all but demand that, instead, they actually try to come up with viable solutions to the issues at hand. I throw the equivalent of an adult, yet politically correct, fit on the floor of the Senate when the two parties get into adult, yet politically correct, pissing matches. I have zero tolerance for putting one party's ideas down without offering a plan that fixes the issue that started the argument to begin with. Either give us all a suggestion as to what can actually work for the parties involved, or hush it. We were supposed to be there to solve problems, not point fingers and complain.

Yeah, people either really like me, or they really, really can't stand me. But, hey, you try getting that many people to agree on something. It's not easy.

At any rate, Dad and I decided that we'd be escorting each other, thank you very much. Let them take from that what they wanted, it's just easier on both of us. Now I just had to deal with all the opinions coming my way about hair, makeup, nails, gown choice, and how it was all going to coordinate with the color of the handkerchief or rose Dad wore in his breast pocket.

I just couldn't bring myself to care anymore; everyone had a criticism no matter what I did when it came to fashion. Normally, I cared about public opinion. We're all here to serve, even if we all do seem to have different ideas on how to do that. But I've grown tired of people having an opinion on my personal decisions when my gown choice, or chosen pair of shoes, had no bearing on the kind of job I did. I could *almost* understand why no matter whom I dated, or whether I dated at all, was a no-win situation. But whether I wore lipstick on a given day or not? Get a life of your own, people!

The public may seem to not have more important things to worry about, but I sure as hell did.

2 COLORADO

We were now a week away from the state dinner. And this week wasn't, by any means, going to be typical. Dad was away, holding town hall meetings across the west. Today was Colorado's turn.

I was taking my security briefing in the Oval Office this morning. Whenever Dad was away, I liked to handle the morning meetings in the Oval. In his absence, I took more meetings and handled more phone calls than normal. The change in office not only helped me remember to act on his title's behalf, but served to remind those I was meeting with of the fact, as well.

"The Secret Service isn't pleased with the President this morning," George, the head of my Secret Service detail said.

"Of course, they aren't," I said with a smile. "What's the matter? Does he want to work too many rope lines?" Dad liked to break up the monotony of trips like this. If he could stop and shake hands and wave, he did.

"No. Ronald," referring to the director of the Secret Service, "wants the President to fly from his morning location to his afternoon destination by chopper. Your father wants a road trip."

"Calling him 'your father' isn't going to get me to intervene and try to talk him out of it. I may do a great many things that a first lady is usually around to do, but helping security manipulate him is not one of them. If he's doing a road trip, I'm jealous. Heaven forbid he actually gets to see a little bit of the country he's supposed to be leading."

George sighed and scratched his head. He'd have to tell Ronald that he'd tried to rally me to his side and failed.

"Who ended up winning?" I asked.

"The President. They'll be driving convoy-style."

I laughed. Dad had probably turned the whole discussion into a debate, and my Dad was one hell of a debater. The debates among the candidates were what had won my father the election. He just settled in on his well thought out opinion and used reason and logic to wear his opponent down. He listened to his opponent and noted their concerns. He addressed the questions asked of him and countered each point the opponent brought up. When his opponent dodged countering a point of his, he brought attention to it and verbally stated that the person must not have a solution or even solid reasoning for it. When someone else tried to do the same to him, they were never given the chance. Dad would openly concede the point and list all the good that his position would do as an explanation as to why he thought that small sacrifice was worth it.

Will entered the Oval through the Chief of Staff's door. — It seemed that I wasn't the only one who was partially working out of a different office this week. — "The President Pro Tempore is still out," he announced.

I sighed. The President Pro Tem is my number two man. He's the one the Constitution leaves in charge of the Senate when I'm not there. His absence meant that I didn't have him to lean on, to take over some of my regular duties, while I took on some of Dad's. "How's his wife doing?"

"Not well. She's not going to make it. He's keeping vigil with their son and daughter."

"Oh, man. I knew it was bad, but I didn't know she'd reached the end." I looked back down at the paperwork in my hands. I was going to miss her.

"Also, Ma'am, the Speaker of the House is in the ICU at Washington Hospital Center."

My head shot up from the folder I'd been skimming. "What happened to him?"

"He had a heart attack around two a.m."

"How bad is he?"

"They're still running tests. They don't have a prognosis, yet."

The Speaker oversees the House of Representatives. Now both halves of Congress were sitting without an able-bodied leader.

Well, I guess it was a darned good thing Congress wasn't in session. If I had to run back over to take charge of the Senate, then there'd be nobody here to take point in the President's absence.

After all of my standard morning meetings, I was off to the Roosevelt room to take a meeting on trying to get a flat tax-rate passed for the country. This was Dad's pet project. He hadn't wanted me taking the meeting for it, and I hadn't wanted to. But the people coming for the meeting insisted it had to happen this week because they had no other time available when they could all come together. In reality, they just didn't want to have to deal with him directly on this one. They didn't want his calm, logical debate-style answers that they had a hard time arguing with or swaying him away from. They thought it would be easier to deal with someone else. So, Dad asked me to handle it.

I'm not a fan of his plan. Not because I don't believe in it, but because I don't see any way in hell that Congress would ever, ever agree to pass it. However, I wasn't here to represent my own opinion today. I was here to represent the President's agenda.

I could smell blood in the water when I walked into the room and saw how relaxed they were. They smelled it, too. It really was too bad for them that they thought the blood was mine. The only true shark in these waters today was me.

I could see it in a few of their faces; they knew where I stood on this issue. They thought they could steam-roll over me, and get me to agree to something that they knew Dad would never accept. They were mistaken. One ended up trying to distract me by waving a deal for one of my own pet projects in my face if I could sacrifice something on Dad's list of objectives for the meeting. A couple of them thought that I'd be more wishy-washy about getting through the items on Dad's punch list for the meeting and that I wouldn't force them to get anywhere on the matter. They had all underestimated me. I was not going to let them show up, hmm-haw around, not get anywhere, and then leave with the ability to say that they had shown up and tried but just couldn't see eye-to-eye with anything the President wanted.

They never would have tried to pull that with my father. And I was irritated that they'd tried to do it with me.

The only way in which I ran meetings differently than Dad was that when I filled in for the President of the United States, I walked into the meeting room all business. I had items to discuss on my clipboard, goals to achieve, and a minimum amount of acceptable progress to attain. I didn't joke, I wasn't into pleasantries, it was just down and dirty business.

I'm there because circumstances have put me into the position of trying to do my job and take on parts of his. And I wasn't going to sacrifice my body's minimum requirement of five hours of sleep, or the time to enjoy my morning bath. So, let's all just cut the bull and get down to it.

Some people responded to the change in my behavior with laughter, as if I was either kidding or would be easily thrown off. Others outright admitted they liked meeting with me in my regular role better. They said that at least then I laughed and joked around a bit before I forced the conversation around to making real progress on what could, and could not, be done with an issue.

The bottom line in everything I did was that while I'd had no idea what I was getting myself into when I had agreed to take on my current title, one thing was for sure. I wasn't going to be giving up four to eight years of my life, to this house, just to spin wheels and waste time while people waited for a term to expire and hoped their party's candidate won.

My morning began to fade into afternoon. Meetings had been attended, files read, phone calls made, e-mails sent, and notes taken. Somewhere along the way, there had been a salad that I think I ate. I was also fairly certain the Deputy Chief of Staff had snitched the chocolate chip cookie off my plate and ate it when I dared to take a bathroom break.

And by ten-thirty, I was standing in front of a room full of people, giving a speech. This speech was for me, for one of my own pet projects. I'd opted for lecture-style. I had finished going down the list of the original intentions for initiating common core standards within our educational system. I was then on to how the deplorable implementation of those standards was defeating their intentions, when the Secret Service agents in the room began to stir.

.

3 "THIS IS NOT A DRILL."

My gaze had left the teleprompter to make eye contact with the audience right in the middle of making a crucial point. As I scanned around, my eyes came to land on an agent in the back of the room who put a finger on his earpiece, to shove it in a little deeper, in order to hear a little better. I kept on talking, kept on scanning. And then I saw another agent to my left do the same as the other agent had done.

Something was up.

My eyes went to George, who was standing guard by the main door. He lifted his arm to talk into the mic hiding under his sleeve. No look of impending doom, no hard set of the mouth, there was nothing showing on his face. So, I kept on talking and put my eyes back on the teleprompter to pick up my next talking point.

Then, the two agents waiting in the wings of the stage moved in to flank me.

I just kept talking, having been taught to ignore the ripple of flutters that sometimes went through the team. Whatever it was, they'd take care of it. The less attention I paid to it, the less likely my audience would be bothered by it. The last thing we needed was to cause a panic while the team checked out something that almost always turned out to be nothing.

I was on to my next point when the agent to my right cleared his throat. I turned my head just enough to catch him in my peripheral vision and he gave me a single, small nod.

My mouth went dry.

George and his number two man moved forward from the doorway. They began walking up the center aisle, headed straight for me.

I stopped talking in mid-sentence. My breath caught, and I swear my heart went into suspended animation, while I waited for them to approach.

I've been drilled for this kind of thing before. They throw in drills whenever in the hell they felt like it. But they didn't tend to do it during televised events. This speech wasn't likely drawing a big audience, but still...

It's a drill. It has to be. They're due to drill me when Dad is away, really put me, and the system, through our paces. ...But they do not drill with a live-feed going out. The three internet programs we're streaming to would have a field day with the footage. It'd be all over the news channels by evening...

Something foreign swept over me. Every fiber of my being considered panicking and hyperventilating to be very viable options. I'd never felt like this in a drill. I'd never felt the urge to vomit where I stood before. I could feel the truth seeping into my bones. The dreaded shit had just hit the fan.

I had to close my eyes and take a breath so I could close my mouth and clench my jaw shut. I took a breath and made eye contact with George.

He and I had a deal. I had known from the beginning that the one overwhelming thought I would have in this kind of situation would be a simple yes or no question: *Is he alive?* George was now supposed to either nod that my father was alive, or shake his head that Dad had died. We'd worked out that little signal so that I would have a few moments, while they took me away to whatever secure location they'd designated, for me to get my head on straight. I had to have my emotions under lock and key because, in a crisis, I was about to be brought in to either assist or replace the President.

I didn't want to risk panic if he wasn't dead. And if he was dead, I needed time to push down and bury my emotions, in order to get on top of them before they could suffocate me. I needed to be able to continue to function.

George responded to my eye contact with a shrug.

It took all I had not to let my eyes bug as I drew my head back, squared my shoulders, and forced myself to breathe. *They didn't know... How in the hell could they not know?*

Maybe he'd had a stroke. His Mom had died of a stroke. Maybe he was alive and they just didn't know if he'd survive.

My eyes scanned the shocked audience as the men continued their approach. "If you'll all excuse me, I think I'm needed elsewhere."

I wanted to step around the podium. I wanted to step closer to the two coming for me and meet them partway. But once I've received the nod, I'm not to move. I am to wait until they reach me and escort me out.

I leaned on my training as I came to terms with the idea that there was a threat to my father's life. I took a calming breath and scanned the audience one last time in as confident and self-assured a manner as I could muster. I wanted my expression to convey that *I've got this*, that I can handle whatever *this* turns out to be.

George and his number two man reached me. And they didn't just take me by the arms and lead me out. They lifted me off my feet and, with the two men that had flanked me assisting them, carried me off with the other agents in the room closing in around us. I was surrounded by a wall of people willing to put themselves between me and any obstacle in our way.

Hallway after hallway went by as I tried to get my mind wrapped around what was happening. Hallways turned into tunnels and all I could really see was ceiling tiles passing overhead as the tight circle around me kept us going. I couldn't yet tell if they were taking me to the bunker, or evacuating me underground.

Steel doors opened ahead of us, another hallway whizzed by, and I was unceremoniously deposited into the Situation Room. The extra Secret Service guys that had served as my escort left the room as quickly as they had entered.

My eyes swept the room, taking in that the Deputy Chief of Staff, the Secretary of State, and the Secretary of Homeland Security were already in the room, looking shell-shocked. George positioned himself in front of me, put his hands on my shoulders, and waited until my eyes swung up to give him my full attention. "Madam Vice President, this is not a drill." He paused and waited for a confirmation of my understanding.

All he'd done is told me what my gut already knew. This was real, and I was in this mess for the long haul. I took a breath, gave him my best just-hit-me-with-it expression, and nodded.

"We don't have the President."

I raised a disbelieving eyebrow. I hadn't been prepared to hear that.

"The President was taken by unknown subjects approximately ten minutes ago. The situation is still ongoing," George continued.

"So, we have no way of knowing whether he's alive or not, at this point," I said.

"Correct. Witnesses report that the assailants knocked him unconscious during the struggle. We have no idea how hard the blow was, or if there were any other injuries."

I pulled out of his grasp and stepped away from him. I positioned myself to stand at Dad's spot at the head of the table and let my nails dig into the back of the chair's cushion as I clutched it. "Casualties?"

"Five Secret Service agents, so far."

I refused to ask for names. I was sure to know them all and I just couldn't face finding out who we'd lost right now. "Anybody else injured?"

He gave a heavy sigh. "I'm being told everyone there was injured. When the agents failed, other government officials tried to intervene. Injuries range from cuts and bruises, to gunshot wounds."

I caught the edge of my upper lip between my teeth as I absorbed that. "Do we have any of the enemy's men in our custody?"

"Bodies, no live ones."

"What about the President's tracker?"

"It's been deactivated."

"Ugh," I looked up at the ceiling and rubbed a hand across my forehead. "How?"

"We're guessing they scanned him, found it, cut it out, and destroyed it."

I looked over to the Secretary of Homeland Security, "I want all non-commercial flights landed. And I want a walk-through done on anything trying to leave the country."

He nodded.

I was content to let commercial flights continue to fly simply because I couldn't see how anybody could smuggle Dad onto a plane full of passengers and staff.

I turned back to George, "Do they have any other hostages?"

"No."

"Did they get the football?"

"They didn't even try to grab anything else."

"Do we know if the enemy is foreign or domestic?"

"No. But for a domestic organization to have the capability to pull this off, and for us to not know there was a credible threat in the area..." He shook his head. "My gut's willing to bet big money that they're foreign."

"Was this in any way an inside job?"

"We don't know."

"And your buddies dropped the ball."

"Yes, Ma'am, not to put too fine a point on it."

I gritted my teeth to stop myself from beginning a rampage about how it should be impossible in this day and age, and with the amount of security surrounding the President at all times, for anyone to be able to nab him. *This stuff only happened in movies!* "You'll let me know when your guys track down more information?"

"Of course, Ma'am."

"Have we taken any other hits, anywhere else?"

"No, Ma'am. This appears to be an isolated event. The Secretary of Defense has been notified. And the military is automatically being put on alert to look for any other breaches."

"Is the building secure?"

"Yes. We've also begun clearing out visitors with temporary passes."

"So, I'm staying here?"

"Yes, Ma'am."

"That's all."

"Yes, Ma'am. I'll be right outside." He turned to leave.

"George?" I called out.

He turned back around. "Yes?"

"If your guys turn up any traitors, you give me names. And if they won't talk, you bring them to DC." And give me an interrogator and half an hour

15

alone with the bastard. I'll torture the information out of the person myself, just for the pure pleasure of revenge.

"Yes, Ma'am." He turned and left the room.

I gripped my forehead with my hand for a moment before looking up to address the room at large. "Take us to DEFCON Three."

"Ma'am," an assistant said, "we've been at Five. You want to skip right over Four? The Secretary of Defense is on his way."

I zeroed my eyes in on him. "Take us to DEFCON Three."

"Yes, Ma'am."

4 I HAD A PLAN

I refocused on those seated at the table and crossed my arms over myself in a moment when we were all trying to bolster ourselves.

The door reopened and my assistant, Nikki, walked into the room with the Secretary of Defense hot on her heels.

Just keep putting one foot in front of the other... I turned to look at Will, "Agriculture, Labor, and Interior were with Dad, right?"

"Yeah," he answered.

I turned to my personal secretary-turned-aide, "Nikki, get on the phone and assemble as many of the cabinet members as you can. Then get word on where they took all the injured and get details on their conditions for me. Find out if those three cabinet members out there are in any condition to vote and sign a paper."

"Yes, Ma'am." She did an about-face and scurried off.

Will cleared his throat, "Ma'am?"

I turned back to him and shared a look as we each came to the very real conclusion that, as far as this room was concerned, we were running the show. The two backups were being pulled off the bench and thrown into the fire. But, not only were we concerned that we each needed to hold up under the pressure, we also needed the other not to buckle under, either. I gave him a nod that told him I was here until relieved.

He nodded in return and set his mouth into a grim line of reality. "The Speaker of the House is about to undergo triple bypass surgery and the Senate Pro Tempore hasn't slept in over forty-eight hours, his wife's stats continue to creep closer and closer to baseline."

My face faltered as those two major complications registered. My head swiveled to face the Secretary of State. Unspoken volumes passed between us as the door opened and more people began to filter inside the room and images began to appear on the screens on the far wall.

We all knew the plan I had settled on when differing scenarios had been presented to me in drills. If Dad was hurt, but would survive, I'd just take the office temporarily and hand it back over when he recovered. I would be confident that he would get the best possible care and would be able to just go ahead and step into his shoes for however long a time that he needed.

If Dad died, or if his death was imminent, I would get sworn in and then sign myself out of office temporarily. I'd go deal with what I needed to deal with on a personal level, take care of the funeral and services, catch my breath for half a moment, and reassume the Office of the President. Everyone was fine with that. Even though it had never been done before, no one expected me to be able to serve the role while dealing with so much on an emotional level. Not when I was his only surviving child and he was all the family I had left.

While we didn't know if he was dead or alive at this point, we all knew it was safe to assume that if he were in enemy hands, he'd soon be dead no matter what we did. It was an ugly truth that the drills had trained me to accept, even if I'd never expected it to actually happen.

Because we'd trained for years to assume that we wouldn't get the President back alive, I knew the expectation would be for the cabinet to sign Dad out of office. I was then supposed to turn the office over to the Speaker of the House.

The Speaker knew my plan, damn it. And now, when I needed him, the bugger was in an ICU.

This country had never had to go past the Vice President, in the line of succession, before. Because of that, everyone in the line was aware of what my plan was, so we'd all be prepared for it, if it should ever have to happen.

But now we would be stretched past even that unconventional plan. The Speaker being unavailable took us to the President Pro Tempore of the Senate. But he was going through his own emotional torment and we certainly couldn't expect him to deal with a crisis of this magnitude, either. No freaking way would I ever ask to pull him away from his wife's deathbed.

And *that* brought us to the Secretary of State. And that's why he and I were staring at each other right now.

To have to go all the way to the fifth person in line, when we've never gone past using the second, was something that could shake the confidence of a nation as a whole, far worse than it already would be with Dad gone. I refused to be responsible for that.

But to try to maintain the office myself, once autopilot mode wore off, reality set in, and everything stopped feeling so surreal... Did I have the resolve for that? Could I steel myself against losing Dad, hold my composure together, and make unemotional decisions? Could I? It wasn't something I'd ever considered having to find out.

"Madam Vice President?" the Secretary of Defense asked.

"Yes?" I answered.

"We won't hear from the enemy until they have the President well on his way to wherever they're taking him. They'll leave us hanging and wondering. Now is the time to get the question of the office settled. We need to have the face that's going to ride this out in front of the cameras when communications start. We can't waver in the face of the enemy, or in front of the press."

"I'm aware."

"I just want to confirm, for the record, that you are now the acting president," Will quietly interjected. It was his way of letting me know that while the cabinet had a certain amount of power to remove me on their own, the decision of what to do was pretty much in my hands.

I nodded my understanding. "And, for the record, you're aware that you're my acting Chief of Staff until Henry physically gets back here, yes?" This would be hard enough without trying to deal with Henry over the phone when I was quite certain that Dad's Chief of Staff had his hands full in Colorado.

"I wouldn't have it any other way."

I let my gaze lift and locked eyes with him. That was all I needed for the moment, just someone who believed in me to stand by my side. *I can do this.* I took a steadying breath.

"Ma'am, Mister Secretaries?" Nikki called from the doorway. "Cabinet meeting in ten minutes."

"Perfect, thank you," I said.

"The Secretaries of Agriculture and Labor will be available via secure connections. A team of doctors is currently working on the Secretary of the Interior. They will try to get something set up with him before we begin," Nikki continued.

"And Henry?"

"The Chief of Staff is being stitched up as we speak and plans to be on a plane to get back here as soon as he's bandaged. He'd also like a call from his deputy as soon as possible."

Will nodded acknowledgment.

"All right," I said. "Start clearing my schedule and have a bottle of Mountain Dew and a pack of Post-It Notes waiting in the Cabinet Room for me, please."

"Already in place, Ma'am."

"Call and get the Chief Justice over here and tell her to bring a Bible. And we're also going to need some White House couriers."

"Yes, Ma'am." Nikki turned and left.

"If it's all right with you, I'm going to call him from the office down here. I don't want to stray too far," Will said with a gesture to the doorway opposite the hall door.

I nodded and excused myself, leading the way into the office. I needed a moment where I didn't have everybody staring at me. I left Will to make his call in the corner while I sat at the desk and put my head in my hands to think.

So far, I'd been running on knee-jerk reactions. I'd made small decisions and tossed out preliminary orders left and right, while trying to gather whatever tid-bits of information I could get my hands on. But in a few moments, I'd be in front of the cabinet, asking for a vote and signing papers, and I'd need to make the biggest decision of my life. A decision that would be recorded in history books and that I would be remembered for until the end of mankind as we knew it.

That kind of decision needed to be mindful and purposeful. My decision would alter the course of our history, no matter what I decided. As far as I was concerned, we'd left the realm of easy determinations and had moved on to impossible ones.

Stay the course and face this crisis through, no matter what they threatened to do to my father, and no matter how they plan to try and use him against me. Or, hand the horror scenario over to number five. These were my options.

I don't care who you are, and I don't care whatever drills they may have run the Secretary of State through. When you're fifth in the line of succession, you never expect to become the president of anything, for no matter how temporary a time. Beyond that, it wasn't as if the President had a health crisis, either. This was an international incident. I needed the Secretary of State to be the Secretary of State.

But, at the same time, the country also needed someone in the position of power that could handle this mess and guide the country through to the end. That was the whole purpose in having a number two person to begin with. Which brought me back to; could I do this under these circumstances? Could I stand firm in choosing the good of the country over the good of my father, the one who was responsible for all that I am, and all that I have? I thought I knew, but I had no way to be certain.

Will was still on the phone, quietly talking with Henry. They both knew that as far as my taking over the office was concerned, they'd both stay on in their current positions. What they didn't know was if anyone else would keep them on through the crisis, or toss them out at the start. They didn't know if they were in this for the duration or not.

Will ended the conversation and got off the phone.

"Henry's getting ready to leave the hospital now," he said.

"Good."

"Do you want me to go, so you can have a moment?"

"No. Don't leave me alone in any room, okay?"

His eyes softened and he nodded. "Okay."

I was the type that panicked, or reacted, or cried, or whatever, after the fact. Leaving me alone in a room could trigger that response in me. I was good in the middle of a crisis, and then melted down once my brain had a chance to stop thinking and get quiet. My guard would drop, the tension would ease, and I'd start crying hysterically. And right now, I just frankly didn't have time for that. I had to stomp down all of my emotions, think with my head, and leave my heart under a pile of rubble. There was a real potential for World War III to break out today. I couldn't afford an emotional breakdown.

"Need a hug?" he asked.

I nodded my head, but I didn't move toward him. I wasn't sure how my tear ducts would react to a comforting touch.

He came to me and wrapped his arms around me, holding me tight, and kissed the top of my head. "You can do this," he whispered.

"Which part?"

"All of it, any of it. You can walk in there and face the cabinet. You can sign him out. You can raise your right hand and be sworn in. And you can either bring yourself to sign out and step down, or you can gather yourself together and stay to deal with this. You can do anything, you're that good."

"Are you really trying to give me a pep talk?"

"You can handle this," he insisted. "Henry and I will support your decision, no matter what you choose. And we'll be the first ones to let you know if you start slipping."

"I can only slip if I stay in office."

"No, that's not true. I know you. If you sign yourself out, you're going to have just as hard a time with staying out of here and being in the dark on matters. You're not going to handle not knowing what's going on every second of every minute very well. You know you're not. Someone's going to have to babysit you to keep you out of the way, to keep you from trying to get information and tossing your opinions into the mix. You're a doer, not a watcher. Someone will have to sedate you I'm sure. And you'll still be second-guessing every decision that's made."

"You think I should stay."

"And watch them wave Daddy around in front of you and see you be tortured? Listen to you second-guess yourself for years to come? See you blame yourself for his death, even though you didn't do it and there was nothing else you could have done to stop it?"

I scrunched my face and looked away.

"You're in a no-win situation, sweetheart. There is no one choice that's better than the other from your position as a daughter. You have to ask yourself what's better for the country and then do it. The government has to be stabilized, now."

I nodded and headed for the door. Three cabinet secretaries and the Deputy Chief of Staff gathered behind me, as I walked through the Situation Room, and followed me out.

5 PLAN DEVIATION

Representatives for the Speaker and the President Pro Tem flanked the doors to the Cabinet Room as we approached.

"Madam Vice President," the Speaker's representative began. "The Speaker has been made aware of the situation and refuses to go into surgery until he receives the written declaration from you that the President is unable to hold office. He wishes you to know that under his current circumstances, he cannot adhere to the original plan. He's awaiting your letter of self-removal from office so he can send over his written declaration that he, too, is unable to serve."

"I understand," I told him.

"He knows the position he is putting you and the country in, and he wants you to know that if the doctor wasn't threatening an eminent future on life support, he'd postpone the surgery and be in here."

"I know he would. No one is blaming him for his heart's terrible timing."

"Madam Vice President," the President Pro Tempore's representative said, "the Pro Tem is also awaiting your declarations, by White House messenger. He's torn as to what to do. He feels he's not the best one to serve, at present. He'll serve if the Secretary of State would feel too stretched in his duties to add Presidential ones onto his plate right now. But he also worries the cabinet would feel he isn't fit for the position, either."

The Pro Tem wasn't the only one who'd be worried about his split focus. We'd pretty much already counted both number three and number four in the line-up out of the equation. "How close is his wife to the end?"

"They think sometime today or tomorrow, Ma'am."

"Tell him to stay put. He's where he needs to be."

"Yes, Ma'am."

One of the military guards opened the door for me, and those already assembled inside stood. On the wall were three screens, each showing a live feed for each of our missing cabinet members, in various states of hospital garb.

"Ma'am," the Attorney General gestured to a leather-bound folder on the table. "I have all manner of forms you may need here."

"And do you have all manner of answers to my Constitutional questions as well?"

"It gets kind of vague, Ma'am. We'll do our best to not break it, if we have to stretch her wings a bit."

I gestured around the table as I skipped my normal seat and aimed for the head of the table. "Let's all be seated." We took our respective places and sat. "Let's get right into this. Is anyone not aware of the President's kidnapping and why I have gathered all of you here?"

No one raised a hand or said a word. They all knew what was happening.

"Is there anyone not aware of the Speaker's heart attack early this morning, or the President Pro Tempore's current situation with his wife?"

Again, no one said anything.

"We have no way of knowing if the President is alive, let alone what kind of condition he is in," I said. "Surely we can agree the President cannot be held accountable for executing his duties while in the hands of our enemies. We can't trust whatever orders he may give when there is a gun pressed to his head. He is clearly under duress."

"Ma'am," the Secretary of Agriculture spoke through the speakers of the computer screen, "we realize you're leading up to asking us for a vote to relieve the President of his duties, so you can officially assume the role. But my concern is that all paperwork must be signed by hand and three of us aren't there in person. How does the Constitution attempt to account for the missing signatures?"

"We're all aware the Constitution doesn't factor in technological advances and would not recognize digital signatures. But the twenty-fifth amendment only calls for a majority of the cabinet's signatures. We have twelve out of fifteen members here. We can still do this, though I'm sure we all respect the right of the three of you to voice your opinions on the matter."

The Secretary of Housing and Urban Development spoke next, "We understand that the President has been compromised. You've already been granted, and have assumed, the role of Acting President. Why can we not leave it at that? Why go to the extent of voting him out and swearing you in?"

"It's about the public face of the office and the enemy's level of confidence," the Secretary of Defense answered. "The American people aren't going to be satisfied with an Acting President running things, once they find out about this. And the press will find out soon and spread the word. It's not as though the President has the flu and we can just push all major issues aside for a day or two. This is going to get very public, very fast. The people are going to want a clear leader. Besides, we can't get into a situation where the enemy forces the President to address other world leaders. And we certainly can't have those leaders either unaware he no longer has the seat of power, or unsure as to which person they should actually be listening to. The severity of the situation is such that we need to show people we're still in control of our own government. Voting him out is decisive and bold and clearly understood."

"In light of the severity of the situation, the history we're about to make, and our reduced number of present members, I'm asking all of you to make this a unanimous decision," I said. "Though I have no power or authority to tell you how to vote, I'd like the press to be able to report that we are all in agreement. It will cut down on the debate amongst the people and send a message to our enemy that we do know what we're doing, even if we've never been faced with this kind of situation before."

I let that thought sink in for a moment before I spoke again.

"I now put to you a vote on whether or not we wish to invoke the twenty-fifth amendment of the Constitution of the United States of America. I request we go around the room and cast your verbal vote. If the majority agrees, we'll pass around the paper for the 'yea' signatures of our present members." I scanned my audience and took a breath before proceeding. "Mr. Secretary of State, what is your vote?"

With a weary, but determined look on his face, he said, "Yea."

"Mr. Secretary of the Treasury, what is your vote?" I asked.

He nodded. "Yea."

"Mr. Secretary of Defense?"

"Yea."

"Mr. Attorney General?"

"Yea."

"Mr. Secretary of the Interior?" I asked, looking up at the screen.

"Yea."

"Mr. Secretary of Agriculture?"

"Yea."

"Madam Secretary of Commerce?"

"Yea."

"Mr. Secretary of Labor?"

"Yea."

"Madam Secretary of Health and Human Services?"

"Yea."

"Mr. Secretary of Housing and Urban Development?"

"Yea."

"Mr. Secretary of Transportation?"

"Yea."

"Madam Secretary of Energy?"

"Yea."

"Madam Secretary of Education?"

"Yea."

"Mr. Secretary of Veterans' Affairs?"

"Yea."

"Mr. Secretary of Homeland Security?"

With a heavy sigh, he said, "Yea."

I nodded my head. "So be it."

The Attorney General pulled out the appropriate letter to remove the President from office, gave perfunctory instructions, signed it, and passed it around. They, of course, bypassed our three spectators, and I watched as that piece of thick vellum paper crept its way closer and closer to me. From secretary to secretary, the form made its way around, line after line filling with signatures. The personal meaning of this moment was starting to settle in my mind as I watched the next pen touch the paper and begin to move on it.

I was about to cross a line.

For some, there's a moment in the life of being someone's child where the parent stops taking care of you, and you start taking care of them. It's a moment where you have to step in and make decisions for them, on their behalf.

For some, it's emergency medical decisions. For others, it might be placing a loved one in a nursing home. And for still others, it might be in deciding to end life support.

For me, it came in this form. I couldn't abstain from making this decision. The paper was worthless without my signature of approval. If I didn't sign it, Dad could still be viewed as having some semblance of power.

This was the plug I had to pull. I had to declare him incapable. And while I knew that the enemy would kill him whether I signed this paper or not, it still felt like I was about to sign his death warrant.

My chest constricted as the last cabinet member to sign now placed the paper in front of me. My eyes closed when Will leaned over and placed five pens beside it. I had to force myself to open my eyes and stare down at the page, coming to terms with it. "I want you all to know that I don't do this lightly. It's no secret that I never wanted this job. All of you know the story of how I turned my father down five times before I gave in and agreed to run with him, just to get him to shut up. But you also know that I've taken the job, and the oath I swore, very seriously. I would hope that all of you would know that I wouldn't have sworn the oath if I had any intention of not seeing things through in a manner that I thought best served the country that elected me. I take no pleasure in signing this paper. I only do so now because I believe it's in the best interest of the United States."

I didn't even look up to gauge their reactions.

I pulled my own pen out of my pocket, signed a few letters of my name, slipped the pen back into my pocket, picked up the first pen, signed a few letters of my name, switched pens, signed a few more, and so on, until I'd used all five pens on the table top, and completed my signature. Going through the pompous ceremony of using a number of pens seemed ridiculous under the circumstances, but someday this would be a chapter in our nation's history books and there would be pride in the hearts of the pens' future owners. They would serve those people as a tangible connection to a true piece of history, for better or worse.

"Will?" I asked. "Can you see if the Chief Justice has arrived? And, if so, can you show her in?"

"Of course."

I cued up the video recorder on my cell phone and asked for someone to record the swearing in. "I want video footage as proof for the world that we've done this."

"I want a few of us to record it," the Attorney General said. "We'll compare footage and use the best angle, or edit them together. This is history, it's important that we record it properly.

The Chief Justice walked in a moment later, holding up a Bible. "Truman?"

A hint of a smile turned up a corner of my mouth. "Why Truman's Bible? And how did you get it so fast?"

"Your father told me that Truman and Lincoln nearly tied for your favorite, but that Truman won out in your eyes because so few truly appreciate him."

"Okay, but how did you get the Bible?"

"Truman used two Bibles. One is still on display, and this one we asked to have nearby in case something like this ever happened."

"Which one is this?"

"It's the one they scrounged up for him when he unexpectedly moved up the totem pole."

"Perfect."

"What passage would you like it opened to?"

Funny, I'd always thought I'd just want it closed... but... "Matthew sixteen, twenty-three."

She located the passage and the others positioned themselves with their phones aimed at me.

She held out the Bible. "Raise your right hand and place your left on the Bible, please."

I hesitated, wanting to take just one second to appreciate this moment for what it was. Cause for the moment and parental absences aside, I was about to become the first female President of the United States. I took a deep breath, assumed the position, and made eye contact with the Chief Justice to signal that I was ready.

"I, Molly Amelia Cartwright..." she began.

"I, Molly Amelia Cartwright..." I dutifully repeated.

"Do solemnly swear..."

"Do solemnly swear..."

"That I will faithfully execute..."

"That I will faithfully execute..."

"The Office of President of the United States..."

"The Office of President of the United States..."

"And will to the best of my ability..."

"And will to the best of my ability..."

"Preserve, protect, and defend the Constitution of the United States..."

"Preserve, protect, and defend the Constitution of the United States..."

"So help me God."

"So help me God."

She pulled the Bible away and reached out to shake my hand. She pumped up and down and smiled broadly. "Congratulations, Madam President."

Madam President... "Thank you, Madam Chief Justice."

"Thank you." She took the hint, turned to acknowledge the others, and took her leave.

I sat and then they sat. Then they all stared at me and I stared at them.

"Ma'am," the Attorney General said. "The expectation is that you would now turn the office over and we'll swear in the next in line."

I turned my eyes to him. "The next in line is unavailable. The next in line after him is unavailable. Once this news makes the international circuit, the Secretary of State is going to have his hands beyond full. Do we really want to shake things up more than they already are?"

"But, Ma'am, with all due respect, can you really serve, given our present circumstances? And more importantly, do you really expect us to believe that you can? They have your father. He's your only immediate family member."

I addressed the gathering as a whole. "How did our enemy know Dad would be there? How did they pick the exact right time to strike that would throw us off kilter like we've never been thrown before? How could they pick him out of the group when his mode of transportation wasn't decided upon until the last minute? How much of a coincidence is it that the enemy struck just hours after the Speaker was taken out of commission? And how lucky for them is it that the President Pro Tempore is otherwise occupied?"

"You think we have a traitor on the inside?" the Secretary of Homeland Security asked.

I nodded. "I think we have a mole."

"Do you have any theories as to whom?"

"No. But I don't think shaking up job titles is going to help us find out."

"You can't handle this," the Attorney General said.

"Have I shown any signs of cracking under the pressure? Have I seemed indecisive? Am I sitting here in a puddle of tears?"

"Have you seen your father sitting beside our enemy? Have you had a moment yet to really feel the pressure? How much of that can you take before you shed a tear during contact with the enemy or on camera so the enemy will see it?"

"Madam President," the Secretary of Defense chimed in, "that's not something we can risk."

I leaned forward. "Constitutionally speaking, how are you all going to force me out of office if I don't sign the paper?"

That caused some grumblings and looks of outrage. There was no vice president to sign the paper now, not unless I appointed one, first. Without me, they couldn't knock me off the throne unless they instigated a Congressional vote.

"Congress isn't in session," I reminded them. "Many members aren't in town. How are you going to assemble them in the next couple of hours to get them to declare me unfit, before the world gets wind of what's happening?"

"Molly," the Secretary of Education leaned over the papers in front of her, "don't do this. Don't put the country in the position to have to suffer not only this change in the Presidency, but to suffer a second one in the middle of the same crisis. We will look like we're lost in the woods, like we can't handle it. Other groups will look at us and some will think we're that much more vulnerable. We must show a united front behind a single face."

"How do I know who we can trust? Do you get that if I turn over the office and we fail, I'll do nothing but blame myself for not sticking it out? Especially, when things have lined up the way they have and the timing seems all too perfect for someone to strike against us. I don't believe the best way to find a mole is to play musical chairs with any more jobs than absolutely necessary. The more we do that, the more confusing it gets not only to the public, but for us as well. That piece of parchment we all live and die by gets very vague, very fast the further we spin this out. And the more off balance we are, the more opportunity people have to get to us, betray us, and defeat us."

The Secretary of Defense dropped his voice down a notch, "And once it hits you, the full extent of what has happened to your father, you will falter."

"Really? What makes you think so?"

"You've always said you couldn't."

"I've always said that I wouldn't want to, and I don't. But I don't think my wants matter right now. This is the situation we're in, and the situation he's in, and I can't in any good conscience walk away from this problem. The House is going to have to make decisions about not having a Speaker, or a Vice President, or a President Pro Tempore. People are going to be scrambling in that branch. Do you really want people to be scrambling in this branch, too? The Secretary of State hasn't been properly trained or drilled for this position.

"Plus," I continued, "do we really want the Secretary of State trying to balance two jobs while figuring out what he's supposed to delegate, or how to replace himself with no notice, when it's never been done like this before? There is no deputy or vice for his title, and no one else has spent the time he has cultivating relationships with the other heads of state and their direct representatives. And we certainly can't have his chair empty at a time like this."

"That's politics. We're talking about naked human emotion. How in the hell are you going to handle this as his daughter?" the Secretary of Defense asked.

I sighed. I'd been asking myself that very same question since my gut had started churning back in the room I'd been giving the speech in. "It's gotten very simple in my mind. My father never turned his back on me in my entire life, and I find that I'm now incapable of turning mine on him. I can't bring myself to walk away with this situation unresolved."

"So," the Secretary of State, who actually was the one that had all the right in the world to be questioning my intentions because I was determining his role in this mess, said, "it comes down to fight or flight."

I hadn't thought about it like that. "Yes, and everything in me is telling me to stand and fight. The idea of stepping aside, under these circumstances, is unacceptable to me."

"The idea of you staying makes me nervous," the Secretary of Agriculture stated over the monitor.

"I'll tell you what. If I start making decisions that feel emotional to you, ask me for my reasoning. If I can give you logical reasons that take into consideration other options, then leave me be. If I can't, call me out on it. If I can't correct it, I will sign myself out. In the meantime, we make the Secretary of State a very visible member of our team. He'll be in the wings of any press statements I make, and any other communications he wants to be present for. We'll even let him issue a small statement here and there. We plant a subliminal message of authority. So, if we do need to transition over, it's more palatable to everyone involved. I won't make you go to Congress over it, if I crack. I'll step aside, instead of forcing you all to make an even bigger mess of the Congressional situation."

"I'm in agreement," the Secretary of State declared. "I'd like to be able to maintain focus on the job I'm trained and prepared for. Let's let her handle it. If she can manage to not waver in the face of her personal crisis, it'll go a long way in showing our solidarity as a nation."

The Secretary of Defense nodded, seeming to mull over the options, and finally addressed the rest of the cabinet. "We'll keep an eye on her. She's always brought sound opinions to the table before. The President has always trusted her with matters, and I trusted him. Let's find out what our new President is made of."

It was time to get out while the getting was good. There was no acknowledgement of a consensus, but I wasn't going to wait around and give someone the chance to bring the conversation about me back into the shadow of doubt. I gave the team a nod, asked the Attorney General to get copies of the declaration out to the couriers for delivery, stood up, and walked out.

6 WHO'S YOUR DADDY?

Dad's Press Secretary was waiting at the door of the Situation Room when I got back there. "Are you the President now?"

"Yes."

"Are you going to stay that way?"

"Yes."

She nodded to herself and plowed into her reason for being down here. "Madam President, you need to seriously think about addressing the nation and delivering the news before someone finds out from another source."

"She's right, Ma'am," the Secretary of Defense added. "God forbid the enemy sends out a televised message showing the... uh, former President. If they find out from the enemy first, it will put us on the defense with our own country."

When were we ever not on the defense with our own country?

"Your real problem is the hospital in Colorado," the Press Secretary said.

I groaned. "Who has the story?"

"The only thing people know right now is that a hospital went on lockdown. The hospital isn't saying why, just that there's no danger to the public. They don't have wind of it being the Presidential detail because he wasn't supposed to stop near them. Right now, only the local news stations know about the lockdown and they're keeping quiet because they're trying to poke around for more info before reporting. The more time that passes, though, the more likely someone will broadcast something. And I don't know how much longer the people inside the hospital will keep their mouths shut."

"Do they know that the Secret Service dragged me out of the speech?" I asked.

"No, Ma'am," the Press Secretary answered. "The Secret Service shut down the websites they were streaming to, just before they came in. They're all still being kept in that room, in lockdown, until after we inform the public."

"You're kidding me."

"No, it's a matter of national security. We'll release them as soon as the story is out. Then they can post or leak footage to anybody they want to because it'll show that the Secret Service did its job in keeping you secure."

No way was I touching the comment about the Secret Service doing its job today, not with a thirty-foot pole.

"And then we'll release the footage of you being sworn in," she said.

I rubbed my eyelid because I was afraid it might start twitching. "Let me get this straight. You want me to go on international television and tell people that not only did some group manage to take our president, but that we still don't know where he is, who he's with, or who's responsible for it? You want me to go out there and introduce myself as the new President and then confess that we're stupid in this crisis?"

The Press Secretary nodded. "Yes, it's better to appear to be upfront with the public, rather than holding out for information and end up appearing like we're trying to cover it up. But, you know, we'll use other words instead of 'stupid'."

I shot her a look.

Chelsea schooled her features. "Would you rather someone else serve as your Press Secretary? Is there someone else you'd be more comfortable with?"

I cocked an eyebrow. "No, I'd be more comfortable if someone would finish up inventing a time machine and take us all back a few hours. But since that's not happening today, I'll have to play the publicity game. And we'll play it your way. Work up some sort of statement, and get it approved by whomever you have to get it approval from. I'll look it over and address the nation."

"Are you going to humor me by sticking to a script?"

I took pleasure in smirking at her. "No. A bullet point outline would be more appreciated and a more efficient use of time."

"I just knew you'd be one of those kinds of presidents," she muttered.

"Well, I was one of those kinds of vice presidents. So, at least there are no surprises for you."

Her lips drew tighter to her teeth with the effort it took to resist giving me the eye-roll I deserved. "Yes, thank you, Madam President."

I turned and glanced at Nikki, who'd been waiting outside the Cabinet door and had then followed me down here. Then I turned to look at George. "Is there any reason I can't be up and about in the West Wing? Or do you intend to keep me sequestered down here?"

"Ma'am, we consider ourselves to still be under a grave threat. We're more comfortable when you are down here. We'd like you to make this your home base. But at the moment, you are free to move around the building when you need to take care of matters not appropriate for the Situation Room," George answered.

I turned back to Nikki. "I need senior staff in the Oval in fifteen minutes."

"Your senior staff, or your father's senior staff?"

"Both. Assemble them all, and I want you and Charlotte present as well. I'm going to make it clear who is handling what for the immediate future."

"Yes, Ma'am. Just remember that your father's Communications Director is still in Colorado and his Chief of Staff is still making his way back."

"I understand, Nikki. Just get me everyone else in there."

She turned and left me standing in the hall.

"Ma'am," George said, "I would remind you, we have a meeting room right across the hall, all safe and snug."

I nodded at him, "I'll keep it in mind."

I turned and nodded to the guard. He opened the Sit Room door for me, and the cabinet members standing and waiting behind me.

Everyone, who had remained in the room while we were out, stood when I walked in. Eyes darted back and forth between the Secretary of State and me.

The Secretary of State, knowing they were watching him, assumed his normal spot at the table, but remained standing.

I moved towards the President's chair and waved them down in the same gesture I'd seen my father make countless times before. "Any news?" I asked.

Looks were exchanged as they took in what our silent actions meant. "No, Ma'am," one of the assistants said.

"What about news on any unauthorized flights?" the Secretary of Defense asked.

"None. But they did find a scheduled flight for a small craft that deviated from the plan on record earlier in the day. Personnel didn't think anything of it because it was supposed to be an instructor and student. Once a student takes control, the instructor just keeps them to a certain altitude and area. No one saw them load up in the hanger so we don't know if there was anything unusual. Witnesses say they came out in the plane and took off, looking completely normal. There was little air traffic in the area, so no one gave it much thought when they first deviated. You then grounded small craft flights while they were gone. Attempts at contacting them have been made, but they haven't responded. They should have been back by now, but they aren't."

"And they've tracked this plane to where?" I asked.

"They're working on locating the plane now. The instructor has been working at the small airport in northern New Mexico for years. The student was new, though. He only started a few days ago and has been in the air every day since. He had paperwork from a previous instructor, and said he was in a hurry to finish logging the required hours for his license. He had a valid log for his completed airtime, and seemed like a decent guy. The only red flag was his sudden rush, but he said that he had some vacation time he had to use up before the anniversary of his hire date and wanted to chip away at the clock while he had the time to do it. He told them that it was finally time for him to turn his dream into a reality."

"Are there any reports of a small craft landing and taking off in any fields or any other abnormal places?" I asked.

"Not yet."

"New Mexico, you said. Is it even possible that they are a player in this?"

"Yes, Ma'am. They started out just barely inside the border, and they took off early enough this morning that they could have made it to the site in time."

"So, there's no chance they drove the President into the hanger and stuffed him in before takeoff. But there could be a chance that someone was in the hanger waiting for them and forced his way on."

"Or, if either of the guys were in on it, they landed somewhere, got the President, loaded him in, and left."

"How the hell —" one of the other assistant's started.

"It's Colorado," the Secretary of Defense cut in. "Lots of open spaces with spotty population. You pick the right location, at the right time, and you could get away with just about anything without being seen. How do you think it is that no one else knows about this yet?"

"I should have landed all the planes and closed the borders," I said, shaking my head in self-disgust.

"No. They'd have run to ground or played dodge ball with our blind spots and kept on going, like they seem to be doing now. And even if you had closed the borders, they're big borders. If they want out, either by land or sea, they're going to find a way to get out. They'd just cross at an unmanned point and be gone before we got there, or they could take him to a coastal town and drive off with a boat into open waters. And, the truth is, he could have some hidey-hole somewhere and not be intending to move Cartwright over any borders at all."

"And we have a big-ass country to hide in."

"If they do intend to move him, and we block the way, they'd just hide him out for a while, and we don't want them hiding. Unfortunately, we want them moving so we can find the trail."

"Yeah," Will said, "and if this guy had a legit flight log, then he's lived among us for a while. He's got to have a hideout all lined up. They may have taken Cartwright there immediately after, to regroup before moving out."

"We don't even know if this guy is American or not," I said. "And we haven't heard anything, I'm assuming because they want to get him to wherever they're headed. But, what if they're already there and just biding time to make us think they're taking him further away?"

"Ma'am," the Secretary of Defense said, "we're doing everything we can. The joint chiefs are working on it. We're involving every branch of the military, and every governmental law enforcement agency we have. There's a quiet, but methodical, nationwide manhunt going on out there. We're checking out anything and everything suspicious. And at some point, the mastermind behind the kidnapping will make himself known."

I sighed. "Chelsea's right, I need to hold a press conference. We need to get everyone's eyes looking. Someone might have seen that plane and just dismissed it. They wouldn't have known I'd grounded anything, because all major flights are still on schedule. But if they'd known what happened, they could call in with the information."

The Secretary of Defense nodded. "It's time. We've done all the preliminary work we can do. The longer the smaller airports have to deny takeoffs, the more likely someone will start making noise about wanting to know why."

Will caught my attention and gestured toward the office.

I followed him in and shut the door behind me. He went over to the desk, lifted a manila envelope up, and held it out for me to take.

"What's that?" I asked.

"A present from Daddy. He instructed Henry to give it to you, if you ever had to be unexpectedly sworn in."

"And Henry told you to go get it for me."

"Yes. I was to wait until you'd made your decision, and then deliver it to you."

There was a piece of me that didn't want to touch it. I wondered if it was a goodbye letter. Something like that I'd want to read later, after this whole mess, so I could savor the words and mourn the loss in private, maybe with a bottle of vodka. But maybe it was full of advice, or information about something going on that I didn't know about. Maybe it was a letter of warning about a source of danger that wasn't common knowledge amongst those outside of the very smallest of circles.

I took the envelope, ripped open the seal, reached in, and pulled out a note.

Baby Girl,

President Molly Cartwright, I love how that sounds. I knew damned right well you wouldn't turn it over to someone else. You'll stay, you'll fight your way through, and you'll do your old man proud. I am, as I have always been, so very proud to have you as my daughter. It would have done my heart good to have stood beside you and watch you be sworn in as president. But believe me, whatever happened to bring you into this situation, know that my last thought will be a satisfied one. I died knowing that I raised the first female president of the United States. And that, kid, makes everything else in my world worth it.

I love you,

Dad

I reached back into the envelope and pulled out a desk plaque with a sticky note attached.

Tag, you're it. — It's not actually Truman's, a feisty woman like you deserves one of your own.

I lifted the note to reveal the engraving. *The Buck Stops Here.*

7 WALKING IN MY FOREFATHERS' SHADOWS

Will had left the office to get ready for the senior staff meeting. But I continued to stand there, rereading the notes Dad had left behind for me.

Reality was beginning to sink in. It still felt surreal, like I was walking around in a nightmare, but I'd just been brought down a notch. Dad's kidnapping had become more real to me because I was now holding the contents of an envelope I was never meant to see unless the nightmare had become a reality.

I set the plaque at my place at the table on my way through the Sit Room.

I took the long way to the Oval Office and walked down the hall that housed the portraits of the past presidents. It was almost as if I could feel them looking down at me as I passed by. Each one had contributed their piece, however big or small, to make this country what it was.

Now it was my turn.

Some had led wars, and some had avoided them. The coming hours and days would determine which side of that particular line I would fall on. Somehow, I thought I'd end up on the side I didn't want to be on. But I'd be damned if I landed on the wrong side of the victory line, to stand there all alone while my predecessors all remained lined up on the other.

I walked past Charlotte's empty desk on my way through the outer office into the Oval. No doubt, Dad's office secretary was inside, waiting to find out if she still had a job.

I walked in and everyone stood. *Yeah, like that's not going to get on my nerves.* I waved them down. Those who had seats previously sat back down and the others stood behind the couches. I moved to stand in front of the desk so I could lean back against it.

My father's staff stood to my right. My own staff stood to my left. And all eyes were, once again, on me.

I took a moment to scan the audience and make eye contact with each of them. "I'm going to make this as simple as I possibly can. I'm not into playing musical positions just yet. So, until the crisis passes and the immediate dust settles, whatever your job was when you woke up this morning is still your job."

I turned to the Vice-Presidential staff, "I understand that there is no longer a Vice President for anyone to serve, but the office still exists. Tie up loose ends, keep working on pet projects, field the phone calls coming into the office, and start coming up with a list of names for the empty chair behind the desk. Who can you guys come up with that will care about the pets? Who can keep congress moving forward?"

I turned to address those on my right, "I also understand that the rest of you were hired to serve my father. Cut us all some slack and stay on through this. If we work well together in the new dynamic, you'll stay. If not, hang with me until I can replace you with more consideration than a knee-jerk, panicked reaction." I had a list of people I figured I'd want for each position tucked away in a folder in one of my desk drawers, but I'd worry about that another day.

My instructions had left me with two secretaries vying for the same job, so I positioned myself to address them both. "Charlotte, you're still the President's secretary, handle the Oval Office stuff. Cancel meetings, and field phone calls coming to your desk. Keep the hounds at bay while I deal with the mess downstairs. Nikki, continue to be my personal secretary and aide through this, despite my change in title. Just keep doing what you've been doing since this happened. I need one secretary at the desk and another to be mobile. Stick someone else on the phones at the Vice-Presidential office."

I turned and addressed the group at large again, "Once we all get our footing and bearings, I can have a conversation with each of you as to what you'd all like to do going forward."

"Ma'am," Charlotte said, "I'm more than happy to serve at the pleasure of the President, and maybe I'm pointing out the obvious, but you're talking as though your change in title will be permanent."

I rubbed my head, saddened that she was going to make me say it. "I believe it is."

"We could get him back..."

"How?" I asked.

"Well we aren't defenseless, this is the United States!" she said.

"We're not omnipotent. If we were, they'd have never gotten a hold of him in the first place."

"And now, you're writing him off?" She looked incredulous.

My voice turned harsh in the face of the truth. "What would you have me do? Whoever has him is going to use him as bait. And whatever they ask for won't be small. They hadn't nabbed some lower ranking official. These people kidnapped the President of the United States. It's a concept so absurd to our way of thinking that, as a culture, we make fun of the notion, create elaborate stories of White House takeovers, and laugh when the actor playing the President dares to pick up a gun. Because, why would he ever need to know how to shoot?

"They did this to prove that they could. They masterminded something that no one else has ever been able to do before. This is tantamount to a dog moving in and claiming new territory. It's a power play. And when the demands come in, we can't give in to them. And if we don't, if we hold steady against them, then we will lose one person. But if we were to give in, it would only be to lose countless more.

"How many lives is he worth, Charlotte? To me, he's worth thousands, hundreds of thousands. But to the rest of the world, he's the captain of a ship. He's supposed to offer himself up as a sacrifice to save the rest of us. Do you expect me to stand in his way of doing that? If we give in, just to get him back, he'd never look at me the same way again. He'd be grateful that I saved him, but still very disappointed in me. And what's worse is that he'd have to clean up the mess I made, because the office would revert back to him.

"But then again, if we were to give in, the reality is that the demands would just keep on coming. If we give them one thing, they'll figure we'll give another, and another, and another. They'll keep demanding more and more until we finally say no, and mean it. And when we do, they'll kill him because he'd outlasted his usefulness. And between that time and this, they'll treat him like trash. They'll threaten, and degrade, and beat, and whatever else amuses them while they dangle him in front of us. The reality is that if he's not dead, he's going to be. And I'll be damned if I'm going to sully his sacrifice with our ill-fated intentions."

I could tell that my declarations, while true, didn't sit quite right with everyone in the room. But they hadn't been through the trainings I'd been through. They hadn't had the same scenarios and statistics thrown at them that I'd had.

They hadn't been made to face two very ugly truths. One, criminals lie. And two, this country does not have the ability to play God and force things to go our way.

Silence had reigned when I'd finished speaking. No one was able to form an argument against what I'd said.

I was disappointed. I'd so wished somebody amongst all the trusted people I was surrounded by would have been able to think of something, anything, to tell me to do that had a hope of bringing my Dad back alive. But they didn't. They couldn't. There was just nothingness and silence.

"Thank you, Madam President," Will said, prompting the others to echo him and take their leave. He moved to stand by the closed door once they were all gone. He stood in silence and bent his head down to work on his tablet, wanting to give me a moment of peace, but remembering my request not to be left alone.

I walked behind the desk and sat in my father's seat.

He'd chosen, as so many other previous presidents had, to use the H. M. S. Resolute Desk. He'd also opted to keep the front panel on. From my time filling in for him while he was away, I knew one of his little secrets. He kept a pair of slippers underneath, tucked in the front corner. They probably migrated between this office and his private one, just off the room. But they were here now.

The slippers were just sitting there, all innocent looking, and awaiting his return. It was an everyday occurrence around here for him. Slip off the loafers and slide on the padded soles. I almost lost it right then and there, thinking about how his feet would never fill them again.

I slipped off my heels and slid my feet into his too-big slippers, wiggling my toes around inside.

There were a thousand things that needed to be done right now, and I was sure they were all delegated out to the proper people and were being done. Everyone else was searching and gathering needed information, and once they had it, they'd bring it to me to decide what to do with it. But until they did that, I had nothing to work with. All of this added up to the fact that as they were all running around me, I had nothing else to do but wait.

I had to wonder why I had Charlotte and Nikki clear the schedule so I could address the crisis, when the system of employees had all the smaller things on our to-do list being delegated out to everyone else. I felt like I should be doing something in the lull.

I looked up at the portrait of President Washington, hanging on the wall. He and I spent a few moments staring at each other. My gaze searching for a little guidance, his gaze telling me not to fuck up his country.

I glanced over at Lincoln's portrait and wondered if he'd ever sat here with Washington's portrait and had the same conversation. I'm thinking he probably did, a few times.

"Ma'am?" Nikki poked her head through one of the office's many doors.

"Yes?"

"Chelsea has a statement ready."

"Thank you. Tell her to get the press together and to tell the networks that we'll be cutting in with live television. She should go ahead and give them a head's up to round their news staff into the studios. Let them know now that they'll be broadcasting and updating around the clock today because the President is about to break a bombshell."

"Yes, Ma'am," she said and turned to leave.

Looks like they'd found something for me to do.

8 THE SOUND OF SILENCE

It was annoying the crap out of me to have someone fussing with my clothing and touching up my makeup as I approached the briefing room. I'd have slapped her hands away, but even though I didn't feel this was a time when looking disheveled should matter, I knew the rest of the country wouldn't agree. They'd see disheveled and think frazzled, which would lead to incompetent, which would spiral towards people whining and crying about me keeping the office instead of them focusing on our need to find the President and discover which one of our enemies was behind it.

Chelsea came up to me, her eyes bright with tension and anxiety. "How do you want to do this? Should I lead into the story and then bring you in?"

"No, no leading in. Just go out there and introduce the President without a name."

"They know the President isn't supposed to be here."

"I know. I want the added shock factor."

"I don't know if that's such a good idea."

"We're about to go out there and tell them we have a hell of a big problem and no immediate answers to go with it. The least I can do is to provide some sort of feeling that someone is in control. If I unexpectedly walk out there with a new title, we can at least look like we're on top of handling the things we can control. I want them to know we're not just twiddling our thumbs while we wait."

Chelsea sighed. "I don't want them focused on your staying in your new title."

"I do. The news stations are going to have time on their hands to fill and hardly any information from us to analyze. They can fill their time discussing the Constitution and hold their own debates on whether I should stay in office, or not. Better that than constantly lamenting the fact, on air, that we seem to be without any control of the situation."

"Fine." Chelsea glanced over my shoulder and I turned to see both the Secretaries of State and Defense coming up the hall. "Are you ready, sir?" Chelsea asked.

The Secretary of Defense nodded, and Chelsea took off into the room. He turned to me and whispered, "Just don't dig a hole I'll have to climb out of with them."

I shot him a wry look.

"Please," he added.

I gave him a small nod and turned to the Secretary of State. "Just step out far enough to be seen in the wings. It's standard for them to say that you're there to show your support. It might also grease the wheels with other heads of state to see you on the camera when you refuse to let them talk to me and insist they only talk to you when the calls start coming in."

He nodded.

"If you want your presence to really be known," Chelsea offered, "we can have you make a small statement later and update the people on what you find out, and any information you collect, once this goes international. Even if it's only to rule out groups we know aren't responsible. The more statements and briefings we can offer, the better we look."

The Secretary shot me a look. Press statements weren't typically a part of his job description. I guessed it was a good thing he wasn't stuck being the President.

Chelsea went out and stood in front of the gaggle of reporters. They shushed themselves as soon as she took center stage.

I swear they all looked like a school of circling sharks, just waiting for her to toss out the first bucketful of chum.

Chelsea waited until she received the signal that we were live nationally and cut right to the chase. "Here now, the President." And she immediately stepped to the far side.

I could hear the confusion in the silence of the audience. They'd seen images of Dad in Colorado early this morning, and now Chelsea was telling them that he was here.

I threw on a confident face and stepped out into view.

Shock mixed with confusion on their faces.

I stood in front of the microphones, tilted my head up slightly, and let the stunned silence surround me.

I could feel the change in the air pressure as people lost the confusion, delved deeper into the shock, and conjured up an understanding that they had no clue what was coming.

I'd never seen anything like it. They stopped fidgeting. They stopped whispering. A complete and expectant silence now reigned in the room.

And all eyes were on me.

"Ladies and gentlemen, at approximately ten fifty-four a.m. an attack on the presidential caravan was launched while en route to this afternoon's town hall meeting location. Members of the entourage suffered five Secret Service tragedies, and the rest of those present suffered varying degrees of injury. During the attack, President James Cartwright was taken hostage."

I paused for a short moment to let that sink in.

"I was informed of this approximately ten minutes later, after I had been evacuated to the Situation Room. At this time, we do not know the condition of President James Cartwright. I immediately held a meeting with the entire cabinet. Given that President James Cartwright is now a hostage, he is under obvious duress, and as such, cannot be trusted to perform his duties as President of the United States. Because of this, all fifteen members of the cabinet, and myself, unanimously voted for the removal of the President from office. The form that was delivered, in accordance with the Constitution, to the Speaker of the House and to the President Pro Tempore of the Senate held only twelve out of fifteen cabinet signatures. This is due to the fact that three cabinet members remain in Colorado as they are receiving treatment for their injuries incurred during the incident. As Vice President, I was immediately sworn in as the new and current President of the United States. Due to the Speaker's health, and the President Pro Tempore's personal crisis, I intend to keep this title and not remove myself as previously planned. Now, to give you more particulars on the incident itself, I give you our Secretary of Defense." I stepped back and the Secretary stepped forward.

I could tell they were torn between shouting out questions for me, and remaining silent to hear whatever details the Secretary might give them. Their silence was in vain because his explanations weren't going to be very satisfying.

Sam kept his gaze down and made his statement both brief and concise. I've yet to ever see a Secretary of Defense comfortable in front of a camera, addressing the nation. Today proved to be no exception. "Thank you," he said at the end, and stepped back.

The buzz began to build as Chelsea stepped back up to the microphones. "Thank you, ladies and gentlemen. There will be no questions at this time. We will, however, begin a brief broadcasting momentarily."

The three of us, followed by a silent Secretary of State, left the pressroom at the sound of a shouted jumble of questions, most of which we left hanging because we just didn't have the answers. The other questions would just make me rehash my reasoning, and therefore, my every thought of the last couple of hours.

I was guessing that they wouldn't like it if I'd told them to back off and let me do the job they'd voted me in to do. Sure, they had technically voted for my father, but my name had been on the ticket, too. They knew I was part of the deal and had voted for Dad anyway.

Either way, answering their questions would only put more information into the hands of the enemy. Whoever he or she may be, I really didn't want the person to know how I was feeling about the situation, why I didn't turn the office over, or what it felt like to be carried off by my Secret Service agents.

By the time the Secretaries and I returned to the Situation Room, the news channels were airing first my forced exodus, and then my swearing in. A portion of the screened sidewall was showing live broadcasts for three networks. All of them were in the process of broadcasting the two videos.

I could just imagine the hundreds of news people rushing to the stations, shouting, cursing, waving arms in agitation, and trying to figure out what topics to discuss and what visuals to show. I had to wonder what kind of attitude each network would end up taking.

"Nikki." I hadn't said it to anyone in particular, I hadn't even said it that loudly, but someone opened the door and called her name. Seconds later she appeared by my side.

"Ma'am?"

"I want someone in the Press Secretary's office to keep track of each station's general attitude. I want to know who plays it like we're idiots for not knowing more and for leaving me in charge. And I want to know who supports the efforts being made and understands that even if we did have answers, we wouldn't necessarily make them known anyway because the enemy might be watching their network, waiting to garner information."

"I'm sure they already know how all that is going to go down, but I'll tell them you want notes."

"Tell whoever it is that you speak with to list names. As we release information, I may very well issue it to certain ones based on their attitude alone, and use it to our advantage. It may even decide who is allowed to ask questions in the next press conference."

She smiled. "Chelsea has played that game many times. But I will tell her to be prepared to play it again." She turned and started to leave.

"Well then," I called out to her, "instead of all that, just tell Chelsea that she might as well know from the beginning that I'm totally onboard with playing the games to our advantage."

"Yes, Ma'am," she said and left.

I looked around the room only to hear it again, the silence. This one was laced with frustration. Here we were, the head honchos of one of the largest and most powerful countries in the world, and our hands couldn't be more tied if we'd had handcuffs and shackles attached to us.

I'd never known there were so many nuances of silence. I've spent the last few years savoring quiet whenever it had presented itself. No one calling my name, no one asking me questions, no one trying to convince me to join their side or to just give up on a topic altogether. There had never been enough to merit analysis.

Now I had silence and it was pissing me off.

It turns out that I'd forgotten all about the other half of praying for silence. In my bid for quiet, I'd forgotten to ask for peace. The saying went 'peace and quiet' for a reason. Never again would I neglect the want for peace. Silence was no good without it.

9 FOOD? SLEEP? YOU'VE GOT TO BE KIDDING ME

It was going on four o'clock in the afternoon and all we'd figured out was that Dad had stopped the procession. He'd stepped out of the car to enjoy the view at a scenic overlook, and that had provided the opportunity for the shootout. The FBI had managed to figure out that the small aircraft we were missing was landed in a meadow and was then driven under the edge of the forest, and parked by a secluded portion of a river in Wyoming. The passengers transferred to another stolen aircraft, this one on floats, and they'd taken off. Whether or not the pilot and student were our culprits, or if someone else had gotten rid of them along the way, was still unknown because we hadn't been able to identify anyone yet.

The FBI had set up a hotline for people to call in, if they thought they had seen anything suspicious. We now knew, from eyewitness accounts, that the plane had headed north. Rumors of a plane with floats flying nowhere near water were coming to us from civilians in Montana. If we hadn't known any better, we would have speculated that the pilot had headed for Canada. Though in truth, enough time had passed that they could very well be over the border by now, slipping through somewhere along the massive stretches of unmanned areas.

The bogey was purposefully dodging any areas with airports, thereby skirting their way around our radars. It was flying low, so as to avoid any other aircraft radars around, and staying to sparsely populated, wooded areas to avoid gaining any more witnesses.

Either this pilot had an incredible and fast-thinking navigator who had scads of time to pick a dodging, yet fairly straight-lined, route that accomplished this, or these people had studied the topography so well that they already knew their flight path... And that would have taken time and planning.

You don't just stumble into circumstances like this and luck your way into the President showing up exactly where you want him to be. Not in the middle of Colorado.

"GEORGE!!!"

The Secretary of State had been speaking with one foreign head of state after another. He put his hand over the receiver to block my yelling.

George had heard me from the hall and opened the door to stick his head inside. "Ma'am."

"I want to know who in the hell's idea it was for the President to drive through the countryside in a car. I want the idiot who put the thought into his head brought to me, now."

"I'll talk to the guys out there and get it figured out."

I nodded and he shut the door.

I nodded to the Secretary of State and he resumed his conversation. I'd spoken with a few heads of state, at their insistence, since the announcement. But the staff was trying to keep their contact with me to a minimum. Mostly, they just wanted to deny any culpability and offer some form of help. But we figured if a country were responsible for this, they probably wouldn't just come right out and admit it. The Secretary of State at least had the veil of a prior relationship with them. He was better able to determine intonation and hesitations while he spoke with them. He'd be more able to judge sincerity, gloating, and mere politeness. Whereas I would be going through the motions of speaking with them, but would have no frame of reference with them, to read between the lines of what they were saying and what they actually meant.

Yet, if the Secretary of State were the President, he'd never be able to do what he was doing with as much accuracy, because his mind would be focused on so many other things. This was exactly why he and I agreed that our current arrangement would be better than the alternative.

The hall door opened, drawing my attention. "Ma'am?" one of the Marine guards called out.

"Yes?"

"The White House Head Chef is out here. He'd like to speak with you."

"Is anyone hungry?" I asked, my eyes sweeping around the room.

Some shook their heads, some scrunched their eyebrows like the thought of food hadn't occurred to them, and others started rubbing their foreheads with their hands and frowned. I guessed we all thought we had more important things to worry about. Oh wait, we did.

"Kindly tell him that we're not hungry. We're depressed over failing to keep our enemies at bay, and busy hoping World War III doesn't break out sometime tonight."

"Um, yeah. The Chef would like permission to set up a small buffet in the back of the room. That way, some of you might eat something as evening comes and the night wears on," the guard said.

"Seriously?" I didn't have the patience to deal with this.

"Ma'am?" the Chef called out from around the corner of the doorway. "All of you have the job of keeping us safe, I understand that. But I'd appreciate it if you'd understand that it's my job to make sure all of you eat and drink to keep your bodies going on something other than caffeine and adrenaline. If you don't want a buffet, then how would you like for me to go about achieving my job?"

My sigh was heavy. "Fine."

I saw the Marine guarding the room nod to the chef and close the door.

As day turned into the first night, theories flew, staff members were questioned, and word of the improving injured came in. We had alerted Canada and asked for assistance in helping us search for the floatplane. More calls of denial were fielded, more offers of help came in, and no one ate much off the buffet of food from the back of the room.

The size of the chicken breasts were too overwhelming to even look at. And the smell of the green bean concoction they had going on back there was about to make me vomit.

We were slowly sending people out of the room to try to get a couple hours rest in the bunkrooms we had down the hall, but I don't think anybody was actually sleeping. Supposedly, though, the theory was that a couple hours away from the frustrating non-influx of information might help our attitudes and dispositions.

Henry, the Chief of Staff, had made it back into town and was now on a fiery rampage. His flaming demeanor actually comforted me. I could calm down a little because he was snapping at everyone on my behalf. I was still strung more tautly than a bow, but I was managing.

My turn to rest came up. "No, thanks," I said. "Someone else can go, I'm good."

"You need to take some quiet time to let your body reset," Henry said.

"I can't go upstairs. I'll crawl out of my skin."

He gave a head nod towards the office. "Go on through the office and into the private study and lay down on the couch for awhile."

"There's no way I can sleep."

"You don't have to. Put on some relaxing music and just try to zone out a little."

"I'd just end up jumping off the couch and pacing."

"You have to rest now so that you're not exhausted by the time they make contact. Will, take her in there and sit with her so she'll settle down for a while." And with a wave towards the office, the White House Chief of Staff had all but dismissed the President of the United States.

I bit back a retort, reminding myself that he was used to handling the

President, whenever Dad's mood kept him from listening to reason. The Chief of Staff was virtually the only one with the ability to get away with such an act.

"Come on," Will prodded, as he took my hand to lead me through the office and into the smaller, dimmer, inner office.

Designers had created the room to be a quiet oasis, a place where the Commander in Chief could take a breather from whatever stressors lay beyond the doors. And while I understood the purpose behind such a thing, I hardly thought it would actually do me any good.

"Music?" Will asked.

I stood there, looking around the room, trying to figure out what to do with myself. "No. Put one of the news channels on."

"You're supposed to relax."

I couldn't help myself. I started pacing. "I can't relax if I'm in here worrying about the possibility of there being any new developments. Keeping the news on will at least make me feel like I'm keeping an eye on things."

"All right, but no volume."

"No! Enough silence. I don't like silence anymore." The feeling of not doing anything about the situation was driving me crazy.

He raised an eyebrow, "Fine." He went over to the shelves along the wall, lifted a small device, and pushed on the screen a few times. Calm, sleepy, Celtic music filled the air. Will had hit that perfect volume that was low enough to be overlooked, yet just high enough to break the silence. He sat down on one end of the couch, took my hand while I was in mid-pace, and pulled me down next to him. He maneuvered me around until I had my head on a soft pillow on his lap, and my feet rested on the other end. "What are you thinking?" he asked.

"Trying to figure out where Dad's head was. What made him want to drive instead of fly? What made him stop at that particular overlook, at that exact moment? Why was driving and making stops along the way a better view for him than a low-flying chopper would have been?"

"Your father never did anything he didn't want to do."

I snorted.

"No, it's true. Sometimes people bugged him and it looked like he gave in. But you know that's not how he operated."

I sighed. "You're right. He heard them out, told them where he stood, and then gathered more research to find out what had made the other person so set on their goals instead of his. If the people and information changed his mind, then he adjusted his own goals to allow for it."

"So, there you go. No one made him drive. No one made him stop."

"I don't doubt that. I just have to wonder who put the idea in his head."

"They said he asked to stop at two other spots before reaching that one."

"Yeah, and they skipped about five other overlooks along the way. I have to wonder if the ones he skipped were just more of basically the same view, or if the three he choose had something in common."

"Maybe he discussed it with other people. I can get you a list of who was in the main cabin of the car with him."

"I want his phone, too. I want to know who he might have been texting with."

"His phone is secure. You can't get into it to look through its history."

I smirked. "Bring me his phone, and I'll get into it."

"You don't have his password. You don't have his thumbprint."

A few ideas flashed through my mind. I knew where I could get the print. "Bet me."

He smiled. "All right. I'll check into whether or not they have it. It could have been in his pocket and is still with him." He started rubbing my forehead, trying to massage away the creases. "Molly?"

"Yeah?"

"What if the driving and stopping was all his idea?"

"There's no way he stopped and, by some extreme coincidence, had chosen a location where someone was waiting for him. Someone might have planted the idea in his head, in the days leading up to the trip, but he didn't come up with stopping on his own."

"What if he did?"

I bit my upper lip as I considered it, then shook my head. "He never would have done that."

"No? He was never a part of the political game before the grass roots, blue-collar movement found him and he got swept up in the momentum of it."

"If he had wanted out, he would have told me. There's no way he orchestrated this whole thing to leave me here, thinking he's gone."

"Not even if he was desperate enough to want to make it all stop?"

"He wouldn't do that and not tell me about it. He wouldn't make me think we were on a deathwatch for him. My father would never do that to me, not after what happened with my Mom and Jacob. Dad wouldn't leave me behind and knowingly let me feel this level of lonely helplessness."

He gave me a squeeze, and had the decency not to try to convince me that I wasn't alone in the world. We both knew he wasn't going to be able to talk me out of that emotion. "What if it's some sort of protective custody kind of thing?"

"Do you know something about what's going on?" I asked him. "Because I've got a pretty darned high level of security clearance. I no longer recognize the term 'classified'."

"No. I'm just saying, everyone on that trip said he asked to stop. And everyone is coming to the same conclusion, that this was preplanned by somebody on the inside."

"Which is why I want to know who he's been talking to."

"Molly, honey, you'd tell me if you set your Dad up so you could have the office, right?"

I drew my head back and turned to look him in the eye. "Sure, every bit as much as you'd tell me if you'd set this up to orchestrate some sort of coup. Maybe it is you. Get in bed with the VP, knock off the Prez, think you might have a pretty good shot at snagging the VP spot for yourself, knock me off, and then you'd get the office."

One side of his mouth drew up and he shook his head. "Damn, you caught me."

"I know, right? I'm so damn good sometimes I scare myself."

I closed my eyes and turned my head on the pillow to snuggle into him a little closer. He reached around and kneaded the back of my neck and head with one hand, while the other sent out texts to look into my questions.

I resolved myself not to focus on appointing a VP of my own until we all knew for sure what had happened to Dad. Inasmuch as I did feel I could trust my masseur, the truth was I couldn't trust anybody. No way was I about to appoint the wrong person and then find myself in Dad's same predicament.

I tried to relax and let my mind meld into the abyss of the soft music. But somewhere, out there, my father was facing the worst nightmare of his life.

This was why I hadn't wanted to be left alone in a room. Right now, I wasn't even in the room by myself. But without people talking and throwing things at me to take care of, without a constant flow of stimulation for my brain to process, I had no choice but to reflect on the day. And this time I didn't have my Presidential buddies on the walls to distract me.

Images flashed through my mind. Me being carried away from my speech, friends in hospital gowns, Truman's Bible, people calling me by my father's title. I didn't want to think about this stuff. I didn't want to sit around and come to terms with how much my life, our lives, had changed in a matter of moments. I didn't want to think about how I could never go back to the simpler way things had been just the day before.

And then the images of different things Dad could possibly be going through flashed before my mind's eye. Ways they could be harming him, injuries he might have, the despair he could be feeling right now. I could only imagine that it might very well be worse for him now than fighting in Vietnam had been.

At least there, he'd had brothers at arms by his side, working with him. Right now, he was facing the enemy all alone. In Vietnam, he'd been just another faceless soldier of the US Army. But now he was the one specific person who had been targeted. He wasn't *an* enemy. He was *the* enemy.

You know, there's a damn good reason why presidents assembled advisors and secretaries around themselves. It was, in part, to temper reactions with logic and reason. I was going to need that, especially if they tortured him. Images of things I'd do to the leader, and the people working for my faceless enemy, danced through my head.

Will managed to drift off, his head hanging to one side, resting on his shoulder. One of his hands was still on the top of my head, the other resting on my waist.

I attempted to focus on the music, in an effort to reign in my wandering imagination. It didn't work for very long, no matter how hard I tried. My imagination was a very scary place to be right now.

As the minutes ticked on by, I did manage to relax a bit. Tears flowed in fat, silent drops as I lay there, willing my brain to shut off.

10 THOSE RAT-BASTARDS!

My eyes drifted open and something on the television drew my attention. I turned my head so I could better focus my bleary eyes on the screen. It was footage of an interview Dad and I had given on the set of a daytime talk show...

Oh. Shit.

I was up and out of the office and back in the Sit Room before Will even knew anything had set me off.

Henry's eyes flew to me. "We're already on it."

"How many of the stations are playing it?"

"All of them."

"Did they all start running it simultaneously?"

"Pretty much."

Damn it. If it had started with one station playing the clip, then somebody at one of the news stations was earning a bonus for having a hellacious memory. It would then be seen by other stations, Googled, a version of the file found, and then replayed into the oblivion of the Let's-Trash-the-White-House bandwagon.

But that wasn't the case. If they had all started playing it simultaneously, it meant somebody sent in a tip to all the news stations at once. And the bait of the interview was juicy enough that they all grabbed hold of it. It was just as effective as planting a story, in the sense of the damage it could do.

However... "If we can trace this back to whomever it was that had pointed them in the direction of the footage in the first place, it might give us a clue as to who orchestrated this whole mess to begin with."

"We'll find out where it came from," Sam reassured me.

There was a single knock on the door and Chelsea emerged from the hall. Her eyes took in the live feed from the stations on the screened walls and nodded. "We need to make a statement about the interview."

"I need to hold a question and answer session with the press," I said.

"No, you really don't," Chelsea countered.

I looked back at the wall and sighed. The interview was from a little over six years ago, just after my father had first taken office. The interviewer had asked which of the nation's highlights were on Dad's must-see list, for the traditional tour of the country that all new presidents take.

Dad had said he knew that many viewed it as a waste of the taxpayer's money and that he'd rather settle down into the meat and bones of the job.

I'd then opened my big mouth and told him that he was about to settle into four to eight years of an up at dawn siege for the country. Then I'd told him that sometimes, when you're stuck in the mire, it was going to be hard to remember why you ever bothered to do it to begin with. I told him that the same people complaining about the cost of letting the president see and experience all that he was representing are the same ones who would love to have the chance to do it themselves and would never think to say no, if the opportunity ever arose for them. I told him to go, to use the time to reflect on his goals.

The people who complain don't ever seem to want to remember that it's something that presidents traditionally do. After months on the campaign trail, listening to people, garnering the media, holding town hall meetings, debates, and question and answer sessions, it was time to be reminded of the best in the country, to remember what you fought so hard for. I'd said he needed to clear his head and transition his mind from running to leading.

I hadn't been the one that was able to convince him to go, though; the Secretary of the Interior had accomplished that. There was a bill he wanted to work on for the national parks. It was the same bill that he was still working on... *Now there's a thought... I wonder if he was in the car with Dad, or in one of the others.*

"I can't just ignore it, it'll imply guilt," I told Chelsea.

"If you go out there upset, you'll look nervous, and therefore guilty. If you go out there calm, you'll look like you're trying to brush it off and therefore guilty. It's a no-win situation. I'll handle it."

"Fine."

"You should think about issuing a statement every so often on our progress. It will keep our presence up, and send the message that we're focused on the tasks at hand. I'll give this one on your behalf; we'll play the others by ear. A dribbling of information is better than silence while waiting to gain all the answers they want."

"Fine. Maybe we can have the Secretary of State make a brief statement this afternoon, as well."

"Another thing, Ma'am..."

"Yes?"

"People are asking about the state dinner. They want to know what your plans for that are now."

"Ugh. We're cancelling it." I pulled out my phone to text Charlotte to unmake all of the arrangements on her end. "The Secretary of State has already talked to most of the confirmed guests." I couldn't have other foreign heads of state coming into the White House when we weren't entirely sure who all our enemies were at the moment. That was besides the fact that if we couldn't keep our head of state safe, there was no way we could claim to be able to keep them safe, either. Heaven forbid that someone had a viable plan to attack or bomb the White House while they were all here.

And, hey, if it saved me from the evening gown and five-inch platform heels, then so be it.

"There is something else, Ma'am."

"What?"

She just looked at me, unwilling to speak the obvious implication of the footage now playing.

"Don't tell me they really think I'm behind this just because I told the man he should go on the tour. They're just tossing out any possibility they can think up, right?"

"There're noises being made now that maybe you held the accident against him this whole time and planted the idea for him to see the country as a way to set him up for revenge."

I rolled my eyes. "If I was holding that against him, I would never have helped him run. I'd have sabotaged him, instead. The party would have kept me hidden away, reporting me to be too busy with a career to constantly campaign. And I certainly wouldn't be living with him now."

"It's theorized that your plan didn't work on his tour, and that you've been biding your time, luring him in. And that you might have had something to do with why he had stopped to sightsee yesterday, and why you're holding onto the office now."

"So, I'm a sociopath."

"It's not really about you. They're just not getting any new facts and they have airtime to fill. The longer we wait for this to play out, the more ridiculous their theories and suggestions will get."

"And right now, it's my turn on the list they're working their way down."

"Yes, Ma'am."

"Whoever was the first one to open their mouth and start that rumor, their station doesn't get to ask any questions."

"I'll make a note. But that's if we ever get to a point where we start taking questions again."

"Thank you," I said.

She recognized the dismissal for what it was and left the room.

I waited until the door closed behind Chelsea and then I turned back to the table. "Somebody tell me you've found something, anything."

"Ma'am," the Secretary of State said, "We've located the float plane. They dropped it near the eastern edge of Great Bear Lake in Canada. Everyone exited out, boarded a boat they already had staged there, drove to the western shore, boarded another floatplane painted with a completely different color scheme than what we've been searching for, and then headed toward the Alaskan border. That's as far as we've been able to track them."

I had grasped the sides of my face and had slowly slid my hands forward to cover my mouth as I tried to picture his description. I dropped them back down to my sides when he was done. "And how far behind them are we trailing?"

"Too far, and we're slipping even further behind as time ticks away. These are sparsely populated areas. But it is encouraging that we've been able to track them to this point."

"Have we figured out if he's dead or alive?"

"They haven't left a body behind anywhere. Search and rescue teams are combing each location we track them to. Other than some footprints, they've found nothing."

"So, let me get this straight. They left the country, and now it looks like they've brought him back in?"

"Who would think to look inside the country, if we managed to track him leaving it?" Sam asked.

"I would."

Sam smiled. "Why?"

"I'd think they'd take him out and sneak him back in to throw us off the trail sooner than I'd believe they were going to stash him somewhere in Canada."

"You think they're going to stash him in Alaska?"

"No, though there certainly are enough places in the state where they could. But that doesn't sit right with me."

Sam nodded with a glint in his eye. "So why are they headed there?"

The man was testing me, and I knew it. "Because they're travelling by small aircraft, so they have to stick close to the mainland."

He smiled. "Where are they really headed?"

"Asia."

He nodded. "We think so, too. They can get away with it until they start hitting the more populated areas. At some point, they'll either have to stop or switch to a private jet of some sort."

"And Asian countries won't support us by grounding private jets."

"Nope," he agreed. "They don't regulate their air spaces like we do."

"Of course, they don't." I gave a bitter laugh. "Neither do we, we just like to think we do."

No one said anything in response to that. I looked around the room again, as was my habit when I was trying to let my mind switch topics. I was vaguely aware that someone had placed new furniture in the back of the room, but I wasn't worried about the decor at the moment. I also spotted my pack of Post-It notes from yesterday, and a fresh bottle of Mountain Dew. Nikki had obviously been here.

"Where do we stand on figuring out who was in the car with Dad?" I asked.

"His personal aide, his head Secret Service man, and the Secretary of the Interior," Sam answered.

"Do all three stories mesh with each other?"

"Well, two of them, yes. Only the aide and the Secretary remained after the attack. His head of Secret Service died in the attack. The aide and the Secretary both said that the Secret Service man was silent. The President, the aide, and the Secretary were all talking about the landscape and how they were never able to travel for pleasure anymore. They joked about how time off was either spent at home, or at a resort of some sort. They both said stopping at the overlook was the President's idea."

"Who started the conversation?"

"The personal aide. But the Secretary and the President jumped right in on it."

So, did the personal aide start it, to get the ball rolling, or did the secretary jump on the opportunity at not having to bring it up himself? OR, was it just a conversation spurred on by the passing scenery?

I squeezed my temples with the palms of my hands. "So, we still have no answers."

"No, Ma'am."

"And the phone?"

"They found it on site and sealed it. It's on a plane with an agent now."

"Good."

"Ma'am?"

"Yes?"

"Tech says you'll need a password, a thumbprint, and facial recognition. How do you think you're going to produce all that?"

I smiled at him. "Easy, I'm going to work the holes in the system."

"It's a sophisticated system."

The phone in front of me on the table started ringing.

"It was made by humans," I said, and picked up the handset. "Cartwright."

"Ma'am," Charlotte said. "I'm doing my best to field phone calls and put off what I can..."

"What do you need?"

"Congress had sent over a bill for the President to sign before they recessed. He wasn't here, so we were holding it for him to deal with when he got back. However, he's not back and the ten days run out tomorrow. You'll have to approve, veto, or ignore it and let it go into a pocket veto."

"Is that for the new food safety and inspection requirements?"

"Yes, Ma'am."

"I'm familiar with it. Send it down with Nikki and I'll look it over to make sure they didn't make any changes to it since I saw the last set of revisions."

"Yes, Ma'am."

I hung up the phone and Will appeared to my left.

"Molly," he said, still not having slipped back into Ma'aming me, despite being in front of other people.

"Yeah?"

"Go upstairs, grab a quick shower, and put on some clean clothes that look similar to yesterday's."

"I don't care —"

"He's right," Henry interrupted. "Appearances. For the press you need the similar clothes. If you look unkempt, you look like the situation is controlling you. If you wear completely different looking clothes, you look too fresh, as though you aren't giving the matter serious attention. For any contact with the enemy, which I would expect sometime today, you need to look clean, calm, and relaxed. Unflappable."

I sighed, hard. "Fine."

"There's a shower in the bathroom off the private study," Henry said as he picked up a phone. "I'll tell Nikki to grab you some clothes."

I picked up a grape off the buffet on my way to the office. I reached the bathroom and shut the door. The knot that had formed in my stomach the moment I saw the Secret Service agents closing in on me yesterday had tightened enough to be painful.

I turned on the water, stripped, and stepped in. I had to brace my arms on either side of the shower to keep from collapsing to my knees once the hot water started pouring over me. I started taking deep breaths, trying to battle down the nausea. They turned into gulps, seeking air between sobs, as tears mixed with the shower water streaming down my face. I gave up and let the crying take over.

Eventually, I got myself calmed back down. But silent tears of stress and worry continued to fall the whole time I soaped up and rinsed off. This was why I hadn't wanted to be left alone, damn it. Tension mounts and then breaks the second I start to try to focus on something normal, like washing my body.

I stood in the shower until I'd spent all the tears I had. I'd been burying my emotions for hours. If I didn't let the cap off and let the steam escape, I'd blow later on. Better to break down and fall apart in private.

I was out of the shower, hair in a bun, and had enough makeup on to look like I had put a little effort into it. But I had ditched the heels for slippers and had rejected the skirt, slip, and panty hose in favor of pants.

It was going to be another long day from hell. I was opting for comfort. I'd slip on knee-high hose and heels for the two seconds my lower body would be visible as I approached the podium, if I had to go in front of the press. Until then, everyone could suck it.

I was staring myself down in the mirror, gearing myself up to go back out there, when someone knocked on the door.

"Enter."

One of the assistants popped his head around the door. "Video contact. Now."

My heart fluttered in my chest, s*how time*.

I looked myself in the eye one final time before I let go of the sink and turned to leave the bathroom. As I passed through both offices and strode into the Sit Room, a deadly calm settled through my body. The edge of panic I had first felt at the assistant's words dissipated, and a confidence washed over me. Whoever this was, whatever he wanted, he wasn't getting anything from me.

He could kiss my ass.

11 CONTACT

I locked eyes with Henry.

"They contacted us. We have a live video feed," he said.

"Audio?"

"If they transmit one, we'll hear it."

"And what kind of feed are we going to give them in return?"

He pointed to the back of the room. "Video and audio. The camera's aimed for that spot in the back of the room."

I turned and looked. The area had been in shadows, and my mind too overwhelmed with other things to focus on the changes earlier. The small area was set up with a small desk and chair sitting on carpet, a phone, a plant, lighting to illuminate the area, and a random curtain hanging off to the side, so as to suggest that there was a window just off-camera. It was a staged set. To whoever got the feed, it would appear that I was in an office setting. In reality, I would be in full view of a hub of activity, inside an underground bunker, inside of a modern-day fortress. They must have brought all this in after Henry had unceremoniously sent me to bed. *Henry worked fast.*

"They haven't said anything?" I asked.

"No, they're letting the visual image act as their introduction. I think they're waiting for us to reciprocate."

"Must be one hell of a visual."

"Yes, Ma'am. Get into position and we'll put the feed up on the screen. We'll give you, and the room, about a five-second delay to allow for initial reactions. You give me a nod that you're ready, and we'll start our live feed. The camera's field of vision will be limited to the area on the carpet."

I walked over to the set, propped a hip against the front of the desk, and waited as I looked towards the main screen on the front wall.

The image appeared and both my stomach and jaw dropped in

simultaneous stupefaction and outrage. My Daddy, my poor Daddy, sat center stage, tied to a chair. Rope was coiled around his torso and ankles. His hands looked as though they were tied behind the chair back. Bruises and welts covered his face and arms, already turning his skin a myriad of colors. His expression was tired, weary, and pained.

It was a good thing I had already cried my heart out. If I'd still had any tears left in me at all, I would have sobbed them now. It was hard for me to breathe while looking at him.

His head hung to one side in defeat and I forced myself not to look away. Then I worked my way to looking more closely, beyond the injuries, and found that his piercing gray eyes told a different story than his posture did. They were edged in pain, sure, but they were clear and sharp with focus.

I knew that look. He'd worn the same one for weeks after he recovered from the accident and the double funeral. It was the look that said, 'Yeah, I've been defeated this round, but the war's still going on and it's too soon for anyone to count me out.' That look had let me know that he was going to be okay mentally after the crash, and that he was going to find a way to move on.

That look was a comfort to me now, and gave me an urge to give him a little something that would make the past twenty-four hours worth having lived through. I cleared my throat, "Open with the footage of my swearing in, then cut to me. Cut the transmission altogether if I give you a hand signal."

Sam's eyes crinkled with his frown, but he nodded to his tech guy.

I rolled my shoulders back, tilted my chin up, sat on the edge of the desk, crossed my ankles and my arms, and watched my father's face. I could only hope that he could see our video feed.

Up in the corner of the big screen, a picture-in-picture box had appeared. Their plan was to allow me to see how everything appeared on the transmission to the captor, without my eyes darting away to something off screen. The footage began to play, and as my Daddy watched proof that his little girl had indeed been sworn in as the first female President of the United States, a gleam of pure parental pride flashed in his eyes. We both knew that it had been just as much his accomplishment as it was mine.

The footage stopped, I raised a determined eyebrow, and my image appeared in the corner of the screen.

Someone on their end shifted the camera to the left. My father was now on the right side of the screen, and a middle-eastern man sat in a chair positioned closer to the camera. He gave the impression that he had pushed away from a desk, or table, where his equipment sat within reach. The wall behind them was bare concrete, the chairs looked to be made of simple wood, and the lighting was poor quality.

This looked to be a low-budget operation. I had to wonder why that was. Were they low budget? Or did they just want us to think they were?

The man's clothing was dirty and had multiple holes. My next question became whether this guy was working for someone else, or if he just didn't care about appearances. Either way, he looked like his night had been longer than ours had.

At the end of the day, it didn't matter what he looked like. He was the one sitting in possession of the President... or rather, the former president.

He focused on his camera lens and gave me a smug smile.

I retaliated with a look of disinterested boredom.

Dad looked on with mild interest.

Might as well give Daddy a show.

The man decided to break the silence. "As you can see, I have your President."

"No," I said. "As you've already seen, we've replaced him. My country has their President, you have nothing."

"Ah, but you want your father back."

"No. You can keep him."

He stared back at me in annoyed silence for a beat. "Do you expect me to believe you do not want your father?"

"Do you expect me to believe that you'd give him back?"

"If you do as I require, I will return him to you."

"Really? Where? When? Who's going to deliver him?"

"I'll give you coordinates for the exchange after my demands are met."

"No. There will be no demands met."

He struggled to maintain his composure in the face of my denial.

I waved a dismissive hand, heading off anything he might say. "Perhaps if it were possible for you to return him in the same condition he was in before you abducted him, it might be worth my consideration. But since you can't do that, I don't really see us as having any business to discuss with each other."

"If you don't get him back," he said, "you will look a failure to your country. You will look weak to the world."

"No," I corrected. "My father will look weak for having allowed himself to be captured. I will look strong and steadfast in not having given in to you."

"You will give in to me."

I chuckled under my breath at him. "No, I really won't."

"If you do not listen to me, you will be signing his death papers."

I spoke slowly so that dialect and cultural references would have time to be translated and understood in his mind. "If you think that I don't know you're going to kill him, no matter what I do, then you have underestimated who you are dealing with."

"If you think that denying my wishes is something I will take lightly, then, woman, you've underestimated who you are dealing with."

"Well then, we are at a stalemate. You want something, and I refuse to give you anything."

"I got to your father. I can get to you."

I smiled into the camera. "You're welcome to try."

His face flushed red. "Ignorant woman, I wish to speak to a male representative of your country."

"Idiotic fool, I outrank them all. You will talk to me, or you won't talk at all."

"I'll execute your father on international television."

"I'll go ahead and cut all satellite communications to the country and no one will see it," I bluffed.

"I'll put it on the internet."

"Again, I'll cut satellite communication to the country. I'll blame it on solar flares or magnetic disturbances in the atmosphere."

"You cannot do that."

"Watch me. I bet I can."

"You cannot cut it forever. And the rest of the world will see it live."

"What they will see is that I did not give in to terrorism. They'll see that the United States did not sacrifice millions of people in order to save one. You, my friend, will help me show the world that I am strong enough to not bow down to you."

"You do not even know what it is that I want. It might be something you are willing to give."

"You are right, I do not know. Nor do I care. You will get nothing."

"Your banter is wasting my time."

I nodded. "I have an easy solution to that." I made a fist, down by my hip, and shook it from side to side.

Our end of the transmission cut off.

I dropped my feigned expression and settled my focus on the image of my father on the wall. The captor fumed and made noises in his throat as I kept my gaze on Dad's proud eyes.

I wondered if it was the last time I'd see him alive.

The captor cut his end of the transmission, muttering about stupid American women.

Silence reigned for a moment, each of us trying to garner our own reactions. You can drill, and talk, and theorize all you wanted to, but nothing prepares you for a scene like the one we'd just experienced.

I took a deep breath and drew my mind back into the present. "Did you pin down a location?" I asked the tech guy.

"I'm afraid not, Ma'am. His computer equipment must be very advanced."

"They must have skimped on the decorating to fund it," I quipped.

"That's typical of the cultures in the assumed region, Ma'am," the Secretary of State said. "Sometimes it's that they put little store in their surroundings due to beliefs. Sometimes it's because they were only interested in finding a little hidey-hole to operate in long enough to suit their purposes. And sometimes they think the drab surroundings will make us not think to look in affluent areas."

"Is he really stupid enough to think that I'm alone while I'm talking to him?"

"Probably not, but psychology starts to get in the way. If all he sees is a small office space, and if you don't reach for anything off camera to make him contemplate what might be there, he might begin to accept that you're really in an office. If he never hears any external noises, and you never glance at any of us, his mind will allow him to begin to relax and talk like he's speaking just to you. Basically, we lull him into believing something logic says we would never do."

"Isn't he trying to pull the same thing? Are we really supposed to buy into the idea that he's set up as a one-man operation in some basement?"

"Probably, most likely that's just the room they're keeping Cartwright in. We're smart, though. We'll buy into nothing. We'll assume nothing. You go ahead and talk to him as if you believe you're speaking one-on-one with him. Let him believe you think he's a one man show."

"Do we think he's the head honcho?"

"Three choices," Sam said. "He's either the head, the brains behind a joint operation, or his life depends on his success. It's too soon to tell."

"Death *papers*?" I asked.

"He's fluent in the language, and knows enough about our culture to keep up with you. But he hasn't spent enough time living here, nor studying us, to blend into the larger social circles."

"What about voice patterns?" I asked the tech guy.

"Inconclusive, so far."

I turned back to Sam with a raised eyebrow.

"He's probably part of an international terrorist organization. You spend so much time with people from all over, traveling all over, your own accent can get lost."

"Meaning that they migrate to where they can hide. They have spots all over the Middle East. And, yes, spots in other areas of the world, as well."

"And so, this guy's accent has become a conglomerate of all that?"

"Possibly, more or less. He was probably bounced around, working his way up the ladder. And some people never give up their home accent, some adapt to whatever accent they're living near, and still others pick up different nuances wherever they go. The man could even be faking an accent, just to throw us off. So, really, accents can't be factored into this instance."

I moved over to the table and collapsed into the head chair.

"Ma'am, we're going to find this guy. I don't know how long it'll take, but the more you can get him to talk, the better."

I swung determined eyes over to him. "You don't like that I cut the transmission?"

"No, on the contrary, I liked it. I like that you maintained control. You're going to have to ride that fine line of infuriating him, without pushing him over the edge. Continue the banter and power play. Don't let him get the upper hand. Since he's scrambling the signals, I'd rather see twenty short transmissions than a couple long ones and have it be over."

I closed my eyes at the thought, *twenty transmissions!* I wasn't so sure I could handle seeing my Dad like that nineteen more times without throwing up on somebody. "Is someone watching Dad for signals he might be giving while I banter with the sexist pig?"

"Yes, Ma'am," one of the other assistants answered. "So far he just seemed to be watching you and taking in your handling of the situation."

"And?"

"He understands why you're handling it this way. He knows what the end result is going to be, and he knows you know it. He's proud that you stuck around to tackle this. His body relaxed a fraction when he spotted you. Your presence helped to fortify him, Ma'am."

I had wondered whether he would be pissed that I had seen him like that, or not. Some people got particular over what they wanted your last impression of them to be right before they died. I was glad to hear that my staying in this was a comfort to him, and not a stressor. "But he hasn't sent any signals?"

"Only one. His expression showed that you have his steadfast support."

12 THE EARTH JUST KEEPS SPINNING 'ROUND AND 'ROUND

There was a knock on the door, a Secret Service man peeked around, I gave a nod, and then the Head Chef entered.

He came in, looked at the still fully stocked buffet, and huffed a frustrated sigh.

I just shot him a look.

"You people are going to start feeling light-headed and dizzy," he warned. His head shook as he inspected the buffet more closely. "Bacon, grapes, and pineapple chunks. That's all anybody has eaten."

"I ate a couple Mandarin orange slices," the tech guy said.

"I put milk in my coffee, that has to count for something," the Secretary of State said.

The chef shook his head again and turned back around, removing the expired food and muttering about sustenance and waste.

"You could take the food down to the press room," I suggested.

"It's been sitting out for too long. It could make them sick."

"So?"

Soft chuckles went around the room.

"I don't suppose any of you have any lunch requests?" he asked.

We all just looked at him, blinking in passive-aggressive, 'screw you' behavior.

He didn't give us the finger before he left the room, but I could tell he'd really wanted to.

Shortly after he left, Nikki came in with the Press Secretary and the Attorney General.

"Ma'am, here is the bill for your signature or veto," Nikki said and held a folder out.

"Ma'am," Chelsea said, "I'm wondering if you intend to sign it. If so, I'd like it to be videoed."

I had the decency to look down before I let my eyes roll.

"I won't release the footage right away," she said. "I'll hold onto it until they start making noises about you being preoccupied with the abduction. That's when I'll bring it out and show them you're still making the necessary decisions. I won't do it before, or they'll say you aren't focused on the crisis enough."

I looked at Chelsea, dumbfounded. "It must be exhausting to have your job."

"We've never had a VP take over and sign a bill before the elected president was dead," the Attorney General said, drawing my attention.

"Well I certainly can't let it pocket veto, or they'll say I'm a procrastinator," I countered.

"I'm just saying," the Attorney General continued, "if you sign it, and we get him back, it might make it all seem fuzzy to some people."

Chelsea perked up. "If we're getting him back, then I definitely want her to sign it. It'll be the only bill signed or vetoed by a woman president."

"We're not getting him back," I told them. "We all need to get that through our heads. This situation is temporary, but I'm here until the end of his term."

"Aren't we trying to find their location?" the Attorney General asked.

I gave him an exasperated look. "Of course, we are. And when we find them, if the President is still alive at that point, they'll make sure they kill him before we can actually get to him. It'll be revenge for tracking them down. We are not going to get him back alive. We'll be lucky to get his body back to bury."

Chelsea was more subdued now. "If you're going to make a decision on it, I'd like it videoed in the Oval."

"Fine, I just need to look it over and make sure I'm signing exactly what I think I'm signing," I said.

"So, you're going to act on it?" the Attorney General asked.

"Ugh," I said and sighed in an effort to hold onto my patience with him. "Yes. I am the President." I pointed to my desk plaque from the envelope Dad left for me. "I will be making this decision."

I held onto the folder a little tighter, and headed for the door. I opened it, saw George talking on the phone, made an oval motion with my finger at him to let him know where I was going, saw his nod, and continued on my way.

Moments later, I was in Dad's private office, off the Oval. I pulled open his top drawer, looking for a specific notebook. I found it, took it out, and began scanning the pages for his notes that he'd jotted down on one of them that he'd marked for this particular bill.

Dad preferred to take notes about stuff like this in a paper notebook. He said there was something about writing it out by hand that made it stick in his head more than typing them into a computer or tablet did. I'd picked on him a bit over the last couple of years about it, but it was a system that worked for him. And now I was grateful, because I could at least get my hands on his notes about everything he had in progress, everything that I was going to have to finish dealing with, now that he was gone.

He'd notated all of his thoughts on relevant topics in here. Each page was marked with a topic header, and notes filled the lines beneath each one. It was his cheat sheet. It kept him from forgetting any of the important details due to the immense number of things he had to keep track of. And it was probably also because of the length of time he had to remember things for, due to how long it took between starting something and finally getting it all approved in this town.

I focused on finding the page I needed. Otherwise, I could spend hours getting sidetracked with all the other notes the book contained. I checked the bill against both my memory, and his notations. For once, everything looked to be in order. I smoothed out the corner of the dog-eared page and moved on.

Next, I flipped to the last few filled in sheets and looked for anything marked 'Colorado' or 'Town Hall' and found nothing but key points he'd wanted to make during the meetings. My fingers smoothed out the dog-eared corner before closing the fat notebook.

He'd done that. He had the habit of folding down the corner of each page until the bill or event or meeting was completed. Only once he was officially done with the page, would he then unfold it and let it blend in with all the others he'd finished with. Many of the pages near the Town Hall sheet were still bent. But what drew my attention now was that there was a page near the beginning that remained folded.

Out of sheer curiosity, I flipped the book open to that page and found a heading that made me gasp, 'Bucket List of Things to See'. And beneath that, his list.

Grand Canyon - Helicopter
Four Corners
Volcanoes National Park
Redwoods National Park - Climb a Tree
Rocky Mountain National Park
Oregon Waterfalls
Mesa Verde National Park -- Pull Strings, get insider's tour from an archeologist.
Yellowstone National Park
Denali

Memories from his national tour flooded my mind. He hadn't been able to convince his security detail that he should climb one of the redwoods. He hadn't really been able to convince the park rangers that he should, either.

Volcanoes National Park hadn't gotten done on that trip, either. It took him another two years before he made it out to Hawaii to pay tribute to the anniversary of the attack on Pearl Harbor. He'd managed to sneak in a tour before leaving.

Rocky Mountains National Park had been one of the stops that had been cancelled because North Korea began making moves with their military that were making us nervous. He'd had to settle for a lower than normal fly-over in Air Force One.

This is my fault, I thought as I buried my face in my hands in an effort to pull myself together. I'd been the one to tell him to make a list of things he'd wanted to see. I'd been trying to convince him to take the damned tour. I just thought if he could make a list of places he'd be interested in, that I could get him excited to go. I had thought it would be good for him, that he'd see the stuff on his list and he'd have a hell of a memory from his years spent here. *This is all my fault.* "Oh, my god," I whispered aloud.

"What?" Will asked and moved to my side, having quietly followed me in so I wouldn't be alone.

I handed him the notebook.

"Oh, shit."

Exactly. "HENRY, GEORGE!" I yelled, thinking one would be overseeing the set up in the Oval and the other would be standing watch.

The door opened and they both appeared inside the office.

I gestured for Will to show the notebook to them.

George looked it over and then looked up at me. "He wasn't in the park when he was taken."

"Was it a view of the Rockies?" I asked.

George nodded. "Yes."

"That would have been enough for him," Henry said.

"So, did someone come in here and read this, or did he mention it to somebody?" I asked.

"I don't know, but at least now we know why he so readily wanted to stop. It wouldn't have taken any effort to talk him into driving," Henry said.

I removed the notebook from Henry's hand, put it back in the drawer, picked up the key that Dad had in the corner, shut the drawer, locked it, and pocketed the key. I stood and shooed everyone into the Oval Office and took my place behind the desk.

"Are you signing or vetoing?" Henry asked.

"Signing."

"I'm worried there's a conflict of interest," the Attorney General said. "You were overseeing Congress while this was being written."

I turned and gave him an irritated look. "Are you okay? Can you handle your job right now? Because you seem to be worried about everything and sure of nothing."

His eyes widened before they narrowed on me.

"What would you have me do?" I asked him. "I didn't pioneer this bill, I didn't fight for it, all I tried to do was keep it true to the goal of reducing the number of chemicals Americans put into their bodies in the name of food preservation. All I'm doing at the moment is taking care of one of the responsibilities of my new job title."

He was still looking uneasy.

"What am I doing wrong? Did we not follow the Constitution?"

He sighed. "I'm just worried about a few months from now, when you're sitting here signing the education bill."

"You mean my education bill. The one I've been working on and pushing for since we got into office. I can pretty much kiss that goodbye. They'll take it and rip it apart, changing everything in it, without me there. Then they'll send it over and I'll veto it. I can see it now; headlines will be made about how I vetoed my own bill."

He shook his head. "Go ahead, sign it. I'll just have to spend a few hours doing phone interviews, justifying your right to do so."

Henry intervened, "The entire rest of this Presidential term is going to be spent trying to justify her every action. Welcome to our new reality."

Nikki had gone into the private office to retrieve the bill and now placed it in front of me, and then laid ten pens to my right.

"No," I said.

She paused and drew her hands back, "No, what, Ma'am?"

"One pen. My pen."

"But you're making history."

"Yes, I am. And I'm not about to cheapen it by having ten people and museums being able to claim they have the pen I signed my first bill with. I want my pen." I felt around in my pocket. "I left it on the coffee table in the Sit Room's private office. I took it out when I laid down last night."

"I'll go downstairs and retrieve it for you," she said, and left.

When I was a kid, I went on a field trip to Philadelphia. We walked through all the historic buildings where this country was formed. We sat where our forefathers had sat in Independence Hall. I had been nine, and I'd had very little appreciation for it. — It's not as if I knew I'd be a future President and was standing in my predecessor's footsteps. — I was more interested in the Franklin Institute. More specifically, I was interested in their gift shop.

They had a pen in there like the ones the astronauts used. I was infatuated with the idea of going into outer space. I had to have one of their pens, and some of the dehydrated ice cream they ate up there, too. They were the only things I bought on that field trip. Forget the copies of the Declaration of Independence, or two-inch replicas of the Liberty Bell.

I'd proudly used my astronaut pen to take hard tests with, and to write what seemed to be endlessly long five paragraph essays. As I had gotten older, I brought it out for finals week and for writing term papers. I've used that pen to sign every official document that I've ever signed in my life, including those first few letters of yesterday's signature. And now, I was going to use it to change a law in our country.

Me. I was going to change a law.

I mean, I know it's not really me doing it. Congress was doing it. Still, I'm the implementation of the system of checks and balances. I have a piece of this history, I was going to approve the change, and I was going to do it with *my* pen.

Henry looked on with a baffled face.

I shrugged my shoulders. "I played the pen game with the Presidential forms. This one is mine."

"Why?" he asked.

"Because, in times like these it shouldn't be about pomp and circumstance, it should be about taking care of the country. It's time to keep things rolling, not show off. I'm not flipping through ten pens in front of a camera and then try and play it off like I'm focused on all things important."

Nikki walked back in and handed the pen to me.

I nodded my thanks, gestured for the camera to start recording, waited for the red light to come on, then signed the paper.

Will waited until the red light went off before smiling. "The Smithsonian is all but going to demand that pen at some point, if they ever get wind of everything you've done with it."

I looked at him from the corner of my eye and gave him a sly smile. "It's already in my will to bury it with me."

"Why?" he asked.

"Because it's my history and I'm going to keep this piece of it."

I spent another hour in the Oval, along with a number of Post-It notes that Nikki had handed to me, attempting to take care of a few other things that couldn't be kept waiting much longer.

I took a quick meeting to make sure communications between the branches of government were continuing, and was asked if I knew whom I would be appointing as my Vice. *Um, no.*

I made a phone call to the President Pro Tem, expressing my sincerest condolences on the passing of his wife. A patient, understanding, and caring woman if I'd ever met one. The planet had lost an angel in my eyes.

Charlotte got a call from the party chair, demanding to talk to me. I knew what he wanted. He was going to try to talk me into running for my own term. I dialed the number to return the call, asked his secretary to put me through to his voice mail, and left him a message instructing him to kiss my ass.

Then I finally put my big-girl panties on and called the families of the five Secret Service agents who'd died yesterday while trying to save my father's life. They were the most humbling five experiences of my lifetime. I imagined they'd put the phone in the hands of the family member who had their emotions intact enough to still be kind. They were gracious, and had wished me luck.

The first call had been to the victim's wife. She had tried to put a positive outlook on it. But I wondered if she was just going through the motions for the sake of the four children she was now responsible for raising on her own.

On the second call, the victim's brother said that once I found out who had done it, he wanted me to go to war with them. If I did that, he'd go sign up for whichever military branch would put him on the front lines.

The third call reached another brother, a very scary-talented individual speaking to me on a satellite phone from the middle of a rain forest while on his latest assignment. He simply requested, through gritted teeth, that when I had a name, to call him, and he'd take care of it. I shivered and smiled when I got off the phone with him. I was very thankful that the man was a decorated part of our own special forces, because I sure wouldn't want to be his enemy.

During the fourth call, I spoke to the mother of the victim and she requested that we pray together for each other, I obliged.

It was the last call that brought me to tears when the father actually apologized to me for his son not being able to save my father. I couldn't believe that he'd apologized to me on his son's behalf. I hadn't been able to form a verbal response to that humble action. I ended up clearing my throat, thanked him, and said goodbye.

Five agents had died. Five. And every single other person present was hurt. It wasn't his son's fault, whether it was his son's job or not. They'd been outnumbered and overwhelmed. We, the families of the victims, as well as the victims themselves, all deserved apologies but not from each other.

Jackson, the Director of Communications, was standing in the doorway when I looked up from the last phone call. "They told me you rolled your eyes at the pens."

I smiled. "Good to see you back in one piece."

"Only took them forty-seven stitches to put me back together."

I nodded to his bandaged arm in the sling, "Any permanent damage?"

"Scars. I can't feel much with my little finger, it hurts to move my ring finger, but they say it should all clear up. The way I hit the ground pulled a lot of muscles and tendons in my hand. It didn't help that I landed on the arm they slashed."

"You're lucky they only got to your arm."

"They weren't after a massacre. They only wanted your Dad. Once they knocked you down, they left you alone unless you got back up. And they hadn't counted on so many of us getting back up."

I nodded and went back to his first comment. "I wanted to just sign the paper. One pen, one statement, you know?"

"I agree that now is not the time to worry about ceremony, but you will need to make your peace with the idea of it. Once we pass through this crisis, you're going to have to embrace it."

I sighed. "I know."

He came further inside the room and leaned against a couch. "But do you know why?"

"Because it's tradition, it's how it's done. People want their bragging rights."

"You're missing the bigger picture."

"Well, by all means, enlighten me."

"We preserve traditions and ceremonies so that we don't lose perspective on the bigger picture."

"That we're making history."

"Don't be so terse when you say that. I know it's a phrase we toss around all the time, almost to the point that it loses its meaning. Let me phrase it another way. We're shaping the future by changing our present. That's big, and the pomp and circumstance is all about trying not to lose sight of that. It doesn't matter how big or small an impact the law will have. You signed a bill into law."

"All right, I get it."

"Do you? Because you don't look like you do."

"My brain is a little preoccupied right now, trying to figure out the immediate future."

"I respect that. But you have to know that how you handle this crisis, and then how you handle the rest of the term, is literally writing the pages of your legacy from now until the end of time. This is your piece of history to shape, and you only get one shot at it. The more you're aware of that, the more you'll appreciate multi-pen moments."

"Jackson..."

"They'll teach about Adams and his son, Bush and his son, Harrison and his grandson, and about Cartwright and his daughter. They'll teach about Washington, Jefferson, Lincoln, Roosevelt, Truman, Kennedy, and they'll teach about Molly Cartwright. You are writing the details of what will become your legend. So, weather this crisis, catch your breath quick, and let's make your legend a good one... one that humors tradition and ceremony and, one day, learns to value it."

I threw my hands up. "I hear you."

"I don't want you to be one of the many presidents who spends their last day on the job walking through these halls and thinking, 'Damn, I wish I would have appreciated it more in the moment than I did.'"

I pulled my pen back out of my pocket. "Do you see this? This is the pen that I use to sign all my important papers. Though I grant you, what I've deemed important in my life has evolved greatly as I've gotten older. If there's a document with my name on it, I used this pen to sign it. Leases, contracts, titles, deeds, any legal documents, and term papers — thank you very much. I get it. This pen is my own ceremony. Now, if I have to share that with the rest of the population, then so be it. But any plans involving my signature had better account for this pen being included."

He threw me a wry smile. "Perfect. You can go down in history as the President with a pen superstition.

"Ma'am?" Henry said as he entered the room. "Your father found this while campaigning the first time." He held up a cardboard box. "He told me to give it to you, from him, if something ever happened to him and they swore you in. I'd have given it to you earlier, but I forgot about it until I got back here and Will assured me he took care of the envelope.

"Why wasn't this kept with it?"

"The envelope was kept here. This was kept at my house. I had my secretary run over and get it. I wanted them kept in different places in case something happened to the building. This way, you'd be sure to at least get one of them."

I took the box from his hands and then jumped when the phone on the desk rang.

I picked up the receiver. "Yes?"

"Madam President?" Sam said. "They're transmitting again."

"I'm on my way." I hung up and kept the box in my hand as I headed for the door. "We have contact again."

Henry fell into step behind me.

13 POWER

I hit the bottom of the stairs and started ripping into the box as I made my way down the hall.

I held the box in the crook of my arm so I could remove the tissue paper wrapped around the item. Shoving the paper back into the box, I found myself looking at a coffee mug. The price tag on the bottom of the mug said it was from Kennedy Space Center. Emblazoned on the side were the words, 'Failure is NOT an Option'.

I tossed the box to the Marine guarding the door, walked into the Sit Room, went to the buffet, and fixed myself a cup of coffee.

"Ma'am, he's waiting," Sam chided.

I looked at him over my shoulder. "So?"

He smiled. "You want to start transmitting the empty desk now?"

"Yep."

He called out an order for silence and gestured to the tech guy.

I creamed, I sugared, took a deep breath, and turned to look at the transmission up on the screen.

There they were, the impatient looking asshole and my battered father.

In that moment, for the first time ever, I was glad both Mom and my brother, Jacob, were gone. There's no way I'd have been able to deal with their emotions through this and have to be the one they viewed responsible for not being able to get him back.

I thought I was beginning to get a small taste of Dad's long-harbored fear about how he thought I might really feel about him. I'd told him a thousand times that I didn't blame him just because he'd been driving. It hadn't been his fault and I'd never been mad at him for it, not really. I was mad that they'd died and left me behind to live my life without the two of them. Dad had at least had the decency to survive. But now, Dad was about to do the same thing to me that they'd done.

I was beginning to understand why people contemplated suicide.

I shook my head to clear that thought out. I'd survived losing family before. I could do it again.

The asshole smiled at the camera. "I know what you are trying to do," he taunted. "But I would keep in mind that I have something you want. I hold the power, don't forget that."

I laughed aloud off camera, waited a moment, and then entered the screen, stage right. I sipped my coffee as I took a seat behind the desk. Then I placed the mug up next to the plaque, right where I knew my Dad could see them through his swollen eyes. "We've already established that I don't believe you'll give me anything. Besides, it seems I have something you *need*. So, therefore, I'm the one that actually holds the power."

"If I stood here and removed your father's fingers one at a time, you'd realize the power has shifted."

I chuckled. "I bet we could play that game until you run out of fingers, and you'd lose every time."

His composure was undeterred. "Then I could move onto toes."

"And you would continue to lose." I started a slow verbal descent from unflappable to menacing. "You could keep slicing away pieces of him until there is nothing left, and I still won't give you whatever it is you want. And you'll be left with nothing but chunks of rotting, worthless flesh."

"YOU, BITCH!" he yelled, his strange accent growing thicker.

With an amused look on my face, I raised an eyebrow.

He stood, kicking his chair away, pulled a knife from its sheath at his side, sliced the ropes holding my Dad's left hand behind his back, grabbed a flimsy table from off-camera, dragged it in front of Dad, then held Dad's left hand down on it and focused back on the camera. "IS THIS WHAT YOU WANT?" He held the knife poised above Dad's hand.

My stomach tightened as I desperately steeled my heart for what I knew was about to happen. I was going to have to not flinch.

Dad's face had initially flashed fear and shock at the way we talked. Then he had started taking deep breaths, having realized this moment was coming before I had, gearing himself up for what was about to happen. And then he stared straight into the camera with a resolve so determined that he made me proud to call him my father.

He was giving us all a glimpse of the soldier he'd once been.

He gave a slight nod, giving me his approval to stay the course.

I couldn't manage to hold onto my smile, so I switched to boredom. "You wanna get to the bottom line here? I have other things to do today."

The foreign captor sneered, "You don't have anything else to do. I know how it works. Everything else is held until you get your man back. They're not going to let you do anything."

The man and his confident assumptions pissed me off. "Oh, really?" I said with a smirk. "I'm already changing laws here. What do you think I was doing while you waited for me to get to the desk?"

"You can't do that in a day in your country."

I snickered. "Oh, but I did. I signed my first law-changing bill today. I finally have a chance to make the changes that I want to make."

"Your advisors and your Congress will stop you."

"Really? I didn't see any of them stop me from signing the paper a few minutes ago."

His grip on the knife lessened. "You don't have the power to make laws. All a president in your country can do is tell them what you think would make a good law and then beg for it."

I chuckled and shook my head. "For all your knowledge, you seem to forget what my old job description was."

He looked puzzled. "You were the Vice President."

"Yeah, I was. And do you know what the Vice President does?"

"Beg on Daddy's behalf?"

My smile was wide. "No, I was the President of the Senate. It's not a title that anyone talks about very much, but it is dictated in the Constitution. Look it up. And what do you think I was doing while I was President of the Senate?"

He didn't respond, but his expression shifted as he began to see me in a new light. He flashed me a look that showed me he thought I was bluffing. "I want you to pull your troops out of the Middle East. By tomorrow."

I snorted and crossed my arms over my chest, hugging myself, and stoically meeting my father's gaze, hoping he was seeking mine.

I got the distinct feeling that Dad and I were doing the only thing we could to help each other through what I knew was about to happen. We stared into each other's eyes, and refused to turn away from having to watch the other.

I opened my mouth and let my response to the demand fly, "You are an idiot."

Rage flashed through the man's eyes. He tightened his grip, and slammed the edge of the knife down.

Dad flinched, but recovered quickly. His gaze wasn't as steely as it once had been. Pain glazed the edges as he kept staring.

I hadn't flinched, but I'd held a death grip on my own arms with the way I held them crossed. I was probably giving myself bruises.

With another sneer of triumph, the captor held up the tip of Dad's finger, severed at the first knuckle.

It took a second for me to find my voice. "If I withdraw from the Middle East, the rest of the world will know it's because you demanded it. Every other country with a decent military will move troops in to counter. You'll end up having more troops in the area than there are now."

"Wrong, if the United States runs, so will they by the time I'm through."

I just shook my head. "You're so naive. Every other country in the world is watching the US military right now. If I move out, a hundred other countries will be calling to find out why. And when they're told, they will rally. You can't bully your way through this."

"If you're so confident, try it. Let us see who is right and who is wrong."

I just shook my head. "If I gave that order, the advisors would assemble, vote me out, swear in the next guy, and he'd retract the order. The whole thing would take five minutes," I lied.

His mouth tightened, the arm lifted, and he slammed the knife down again. "MAKE IT HAPPEN!" He held up the next piece of finger that he'd cut off at the second knuckle.

Dad had made a noise that time, and he broke out in a sweat, but he kept his eyes on me and was able to clamp his mouth shut again.

I held myself together, forcing a non-reaction, as much for Dad as for show. "Don't you get it? I don't want him back. He comes back and I have to hand the power back over to him. I've spent the last six years quietly pushing for the legislature I want passed. And now, thanks to you, I no longer have to worry about Dad blocking any law I want. I'm going to spend the next two years signing into law the bills that I designed, instigated, and fought to get for the last six years. So, no, thank you. Keep him."

I reached down and made the gesture with my hand to cut our end of the transmission.

The minute I disappeared off his screen, the jackass yelled and howled with rage at Dad. "YOUR DAUGHTER'S A BITCH!" he screamed.

"Yeah," Dad said through gritted teeth. "If you think she's bad, you should have met her mother."

Jerk face moved to the camera and cut off the transmission.

Everyone in the room was silent, trying to wrap our minds around all that we'd just witnessed. Many in the room appeared shaken by what they'd seen and heard from us. Looks of shock, defeat, and surprise passed around the table.

I moved to grip onto the seat of my chair to try to stop the tremors that had started and were now threatening to overtake me. Tears came unbidden, and it was all I could do to keep them contained.

It was one thing to talk about torture in theory; it was another to see it. We all knew torture happened. We'd all heard the stories, but not many of us ever had ringside seats before.

I was going to lose it. I could feel the eruption rising within me. There was no way I'd be able to hold it in. I got up and started for the office. I paused in the doorway and waited, unable to speak.

I felt Will come to my side and watched as his arm moved around me to turn the knob and open the door.

I walked inside and he took my hand and led me into the inner office.

He shut the door behind us and gathered me in his arms. "Go ahead, let it out."

And that was it. I cried violently. My abdominal muscles hurt from the force of the sobs. My knees gave out and we sunk to the floor as Will held onto me. I'd never felt so many emotions so strongly in my life. Fear, anger, sadness, helplessness, despair, loneliness, rage, they all mixed together to concoct a monster emotion that I had no name for.

He didn't let go until a few minutes after I was done. He was trying to give me time in his protective embrace to let me gather up my tattered resolve so I could continue. He finally pulled away from me, but kept his hands on my shoulders, to look at me. "You okay?"

"No."

"You still determined to see this through?"

"Yes."

"You might want to consider how much more bluffing you want to do. You're going to end up turning suspicion onto yourself."

"If I haven't already accomplished that with my little tirade, then no one else is doing their job."

14 REPERCUSSIONS

When I went back into the Sit Room, there was silence and food awaiting me.

I think the silence was because no one knew what to say to me after all that had transpired. Or maybe they didn't know if I'd go ahead with the whole mess after what we'd just witnessed.

Small plates of food sat on the massive table, each pushed towards the middle so as not to be right in front of you when you sat. They were out of the way, but within reaching distance. I guess the thought was that if it was within our field of vision, we might pick at it.

The food had been prepared in bite-sized pieces, and each piece was spaced apart from the other bites on the plate. There was something very approachable about the food. This layout was underwhelming, while the buffet in the back of the room had been very overwhelming.

And damned if I didn't sit down and pop a bite of grilled marinated chicken into my mouth. Plus, it was less emotionally draining, with everything else that was going on, to grab the bottle of water next to the plate, rather than get back up and grab a fresh soda from the mini fridge in the back.

"Sam, you ever interrogate somebody before?" I asked.

He cleared his throat, "Yes."

"You ever torture someone before?"

"No, Ma'am."

I ran my finger around the edge of the water bottle's rim and slouched back in the chair. "Okay, but you know a thing or two about it, right? I mean, you don't get to hold the position you have without knowledge about the good, the bad, and the ugly of military duty, right?"

"Yes."

"So, if you're going to torture somebody, you want to make the most amount of impact with the least amount of work, right?"

"It depends."

"How so?"

"You have to balance your moves based upon how much you think the person can take and just how much convincing they need to start talking. Some aren't going to talk until four or five moves in. Some pass out after the first move. And some just aren't going to talk."

"Are the moves this guy made anything like our philosophy on torture?"

"No, Ma'am."

"But do you think this guy intends to hack him apart, piece by piece? Or do you think he was going for a big impact from the start, figuring I would crack within the first couple moves?"

"Ma'am?"

I pushed the water bottle aside and focused on Sam. "I'm wondering why he grabbed Dad's left hand. He's right hand dominant. Is this guy trying to start small and work his way to the right hand, which would be harder for Dad to live without? Is it going to get worse, is what I'm asking."

He thought a moment before answering. "I don't know how much he'd think it mattered, if he's just going to kill him anyway... But, if he had a plan, he would think it'd matter to you." He paused and tapped a finger on the table as he thought about it. "I think you pissed him off so bad he wasn't thinking about which hand he cut. Otherwise, I'd picture him to be the type to go for the greater impact. I figure that's why he would have opted for a knuckle at a time, to make the dominant hand last... I don't know. He started yelling, but I thought there was still logical determination in his eyes."

I let my head tilt to the side. "Maybe he thought he was chopping at the dominant hand..."

Sam smiled. "Daddy's playing games."

I caught his eye. "Daddy's holding hope."

The Secretary of Defense lost his smile. "No, Molly, I promise you, he's not. He knows how this is going to end." He looked to the guy who was analyzing the body language, "Doesn't he?"

"Yes, sir," the CIA agent replied. "He gave the impression of trying to be helpful, not hopeful."

I rubbed my hand across my chin and mouth, trying not to display my emotional weakness. "Then why play games? Who does that help?"

Sam flashed a smile of comfort at me. "It helps him. It's a matter of self-preservation. It's a way to keep a little pride while going through this. He's making the man think he's left-handed, so he leaves the right hand alone. It's a tool we teach to help the victim stay sane throughout the ordeal. It makes the captor seem small and stupid in his eyes. Makes him feel like he still gets to win a little victory, it's his way of going down fighting."

"Your guys didn't teach me that in any of the drills."

"He didn't learn it from our drills. He served in our Army during a war. He would have learned the basics of being a captive then."

My voice dropped to a whisper, "He knows I'm playing games, too, right?"

He sensed my insecurity and his smile and tone turned almost fatherly. "Yes. For as surprised as he looked at different moments, you could still see impressed pride. He would expect nothing less than for you to find a way to stall the captor and buy us time." He glanced around the room before looking back at me. "But your games have earned you a lie-detector test from the Secret Service."

I nodded, quickly agreeing. "Understood. I'd like for all of us to be tested. We still have to find the mole. The quiet investigation has been going on for a full day now and has gotten us nowhere. It's time to be blatant in our search."

He made a note. "Test everyone and see who tries to hide from it... I'll make that happen."

"I want non-Secret Service tested by Secret Service, and Secret Service agents tested by your guys. Any test failures, I want retested by the FBI and CIA. I don't want to condemn a framed person."

"Will do."

"No one is an exception."

"Yes, Ma'am."

"Are we any closer to knowing who this guy is?"

"We think he's working either alone, or as the head of a small group."

"How can he be working alone?"

"He could have paid people from another group to do the actual kidnapping. They would have done it for bragging rights, and thought they'd be untraceable to peg for the crime because they then turned him over to someone else, taking their pay and running underground."

"How does a small group handle a huge undertaking like that?"

"Hard to say, being small they are more able to fly under the radar. Keep in mind; this may not have been their first attempt. You know, keep your head down, step back and blend in if it doesn't look like it's going to happen... But..." His eyes met mine.

"But they'd have to have someone on the inside."

"I want every one of the injured tested, before we bring any more of them back in here to work," he said.

"Consider it ordered."

"Yes, Ma'am."

I reached over and took another bite off the plate.

"I think we have to look at the very real possibility that he could put footage of this online," the Secretary of State said. "It could be construed in a very bad light for you, for all of us in this room."

"Yep," was all I could say to that.

"What was the point?" he asked me.

"Well," I said in a sarcastic tone, "I figured if I just simply said that we don't negotiate with terrorists, he might try torturing Dad in order to change my mind." I sighed and reverted to my normal tone. "I thought that if I gave him some excuse based on stolen power, and gave him a phony explanation about not wanting Dad back at all, he might more readily understand that I wouldn't be giving in and spare us all the torture."

The Secretary of State shook his head. "It wouldn't have mattered what you said. He knows the minute he kills Cartwright he'll have no leverage. He's not going to just kill him."

I turned to look at Sam. "So, what's your opinion on what you think I should do?"

"String him along with your story," Sam answered.

"For how long?"

"Until we find him."

"And then what?"

"We catch him."

"We're going to catch him anyway. We have a worldwide manhunt going on. You put that into place as soon as we had a visual and could send his picture out to other countries' leaders. And the other countries will help us because they won't want this guy coming after their country next. Stringing him along is only putting off the inevitable end for Dad and extending the amount of torture inflicted. Now, I refuse to give in to this bastard, but I'm not going to make my father, or this country, go through this drama any longer than absolutely necessary," I said.

"He's going to torture Cartwright no matter what we do," Sam said. "Provoking him and making him angry actually helps our profilers determine what kind of man we're dealing with. The more emotions you can get out of him, the better we can learn to manipulate him."

"All I'm saying," the Secretary of State said, "is that if he puts this out on the internet, or sends footage to the press, we're all screwed."

"Yeah, we will be," I agreed. "I'll be impeached while Congress cries for my resignation. We'll all be dragged through the mud of Congressional hearings, investigations, and questionings. However, what we're doing in this room is more important than our careers, or my promise to Dad to see the rest of his term through. We're talking about the safety of the country. We're talking about worldwide war breaking out with nuclear bombs. Meanwhile, the longer they keep him alive, the longer other countries look at us and shake their heads. We'll go from looking flawed, to weak, to impotent. I can't let that happen. I can't let one incident bring us down to that level. The longer this drags on, the uglier it's going to get for all of us."

"Our careers are just collateral damage?"

I cocked an eyebrow at him. "You knew the score when you took this job. Don't stand there and look all shocked and shaken, now that it's actually coming to pass."

He went from disbelief to turning all splotchy red. "You could handle this in a different way."

I calmly crossed my arms over myself. "What, specifically, would you have me do?"

"Tell him you'll pull out of the Middle East and buy us some time."

"And if that gets leaked to the press or internet, we'll have president after monarch after prime minister calling in here, wanting to read us both the riot act. Not to mention the threats and posturing from them that we'll have to listen to. More than that, he's probably seen too many movies to buy into it anyway. He's probably tracking the ships somehow, or having others track them, and he'd know we weren't actually doing it."

"You could pull out enough to make it look real."

I looked him right in the eye and let my frustrated expression slide into one of suspicion.

He managed to look contrite. "I just want to catch this guy. And I don't think pushing him into torturing and killing the only piece of leverage he has, and then having him disappear on us, is the best way to accomplish that."

I kept my eyes on him. "I hear you. I'm hoping that if he's pushed to hurry before he's ready, he'll make a mistake and it'll cost him enough that he gets caught."

"But if you lie, and pull out just enough to buy some time —"

"The only way I'm pulling any military out of the Middle East is if I'm going to nuke it, so he really can't do whatever it is he's trying to do. Are we clear?"

"Yes, Ma'am."

"Besides, a few of those countries are allies. I won't pull support away from them without knowing our enemy's full intentions."

"In the meantime," Sam interrupted, sharing a look with me, "the Middle East might be a decoy. He might be saying that so we look there while he does something somewhere else."

"Right," I agreed, "making it even harder for us to track any movements. This is why I'm not going to pretend to go along with him. If I do, he might signal for the next phase to begin, and then we're looking for another needle in the haystack. We have to keep him small."

The Secretary of State sighed and looked away.

I watched him for a moment more before focusing on the Secretary of Defense's report. It showed where all of our military positions were, and which ones could be safely moved for retaliation, without leaving a weak spot open for an attack.

The clock had seemed to be at a standstill ever since Dad's finger had gone flying. Now it seemed to have started back up again as people around the room began to update me on what little progress had been made.

"Our technology team is working to narrow the scope of possible locations," Sam informed me. "While they haven't pinpointed it, they are confident is saying the signal came from East Asia."

"Well, that's no surprise given what we knew of where they were headed. Any more leads on their travel route, once they crossed back into Alaska?"

"No, Ma'am."

"So, if he's in East Asia, but wants me to pull out of the Middle East, what's he after? Is it so we'll look for him there? Or so he can tell the people he's working for to go ahead and invade, or stage a coup in, the Middle East? Or is it maybe so he has time to find a new hidey-hole in the Middle East? What's the game?" I asked.

"It may be like you said, if you pull out, others will move in. And if they move in, they'll be leaving previously occupied areas unoccupied, leaving them vulnerable for attack. This may not have anything to do with us. It may be that his interests lie somewhere else entirely, and he's just waiting for the dominoes to fall into place so he/they can go after what they really want."

"Oh, my God. I need some ibuprofen," I said as I rubbed my forehead. *Sooo many possibilities.*

"There's also the possibility that this is simply an audition for him to get into a bigger, badder, organization."

"Are you freaking kidding me?"

"No. He could be trying to get in and was challenged to prove himself."

"So, then it wouldn't be what this guy is planning that we would have to worry about, but what the big, bad, overseeing group is planning?"

"Yep, and by outsourcing it to a young unknown, it buys them more time before we put it together. They might have even given him some equipment or some men to use when he tried. That would explain why we don't know this guy, or have a record of him. The group could also have just gotten seriously lucky that this guy was able to pull it off."

I needed a drink, or five, before I could fully process all the possibilities.

"I'm sorry," one of the assistants said. "May I speak?"

Sam looked to me.

"Please," I said.

"Why are we not plastering this guy's picture all over the news and the internet to get people looking?"

"Fair question," I responded. "I don't want to be the first one to bring the internet into it. If I put the picture out there, he could put a picture of

Dad up. The masses will crucify us, as though we're the ones doing it to him. They'll blame us because it's easy. They'll create more chaos than there already is. And then, he'll start showing footage of Dad to fuel the fires. And that's not to mention all the false leads that will come flooding in, taking manpower away from the few solid leads we do have. Those that we've sent pictures of this guy to are keeping it away from their press and are focusing on having their military quietly looking around for him."

"Also," Sam said, "if we put a picture out there, and admit we have no name or affiliation to go with it..." He shook his head. "It would be worse than our remaining silent."

"Not to mention that he may be hiding in one of our non-allied countries. Someplace where the government would be only too happy to keep him hidden, if they realize he's within their borders," I said.

"Or hate us enough to find the captor, celebrate him a hero, storm his hideout, and burn Cartwright's body in effigy on international television," Sam said.

"Should we keep going?" I asked.

The assistant shook his head. "No, thank you."

People fell silent as we all kept monitoring situations and brainstorming more ideas on what else we could be doing.

I'd started picking my way through the bites on the plate near me. Eventually, between taking notes on my Post-Its and watching the newsfeeds that were back up on the wall, I'd cleared the plate. I looked around and noticed the shrinking numbers of remaining pieces on other's plates, as well.

It seemed as though the kitchen staff had managed to outsmart our knotted insides. They were sneaking food into us, right under our noses. Some of our bellies were primed enough to go get a few more bites off the buffet that was now filled with bite-sized pieces of all manner of things that could be separated into bites without making a mess. I found myself putting cubes of cheese, balls of melon, pieces of bell peppers, and cubes of ham on a plate as I passed by, on my way to get another Mountain Dew.

15 AND THE HITS JUST KEEP ON COMING

I had just finished with my lie detector test — which I passed with flying colors thank you very much — and decided to go check in with Charlotte, outside the Oval. She was doing well in keeping most duties at bay, but there were a couple things what would make her life easier if I just went ahead and dealt with.

I signed a paper, approved a plan, and made two phone calls. Now I was trying to use the room to ground myself, and re-center my brain before moving on. If I could just do this from time to time, I could keep the panic and fear at bay.

All the while, Will maintained a presence somewhere in the room with me. He didn't hover. He just sat on one of the couches with his laptop and worked on his own tasks.

George knocked and entered through the hall door. The look in his eyes was indescribable. It was a mix of stunned, meets fear, meets Oh-shit-I-didn't-see-this-coming.

I winced. "What now?"

He opened his mouth, but no sound came out.

"Are we under attack?"

He shook his head.

"Did something blow up?"

He shook his head.

"We're shots fired?"

He shook his head.

"All right, George, it's been a long day for all of us. I'm going to need you to use your words now."

He took a breath and said, "Jared's gone."

Jared was my father's personal assistant. He'd taken a bullet trying to save Dad the day before. He'd required minor surgery to remove it, stitches, overnight observation, gauze, medical tape, and a sling.

"What. Do. You. Mean. He's. Gone?"

"He disappeared off the plane."

I used the palms of my hands to squeeze my temples.

Will started texting on his phone, probably to Henry.

"What about the Secretary of the Interior?" I asked.

"He's fine and accounted for."

"I need you to make this make sense to me. How does someone vanish off a plane?"

"He... the flight... it wasn't direct," George stammered.

I eyed him down for a second. "You have to snap out of this, or I'm going to start thinking that you are beginning to doubt that you can keep me safe," I said. "Were they supposed to switch planes somewhere?"

He took a deep breath and shook himself. "No. The plane landed to let people off and on, but they were to stay on the plane to continue to DC."

"Why didn't they fly direct?"

"This flight was the first one out, after they were both released from the hospital. They wanted to get back here to help out as soon as possible."

"So how did Jared disappear if they weren't changing planes?"

"He got off. He said he was only going as far as he needed to get some real food for the next leg. He said he wanted something more than the cheese and fruit snack packs the airline was selling. He should have had plenty of time to do that."

"And where was security while this was going on?"

"Ma'am, we're stretched a bit thin. We aren't used to having to cover so much staff in so many different locations, under these kinds of circumstances."

"Meaning?"

"We only had one man with them. We're talking about an aide and a Secretary with a non-flashy title."

"On a commercial flight."

It was his turn to wince. "The more people that fly here, the less men we have on the ground there to watch the others."

"You know," I said, letting my irritation flow, "we have this thing called a military. They can, from time to time, provide armed protection. They also have military aircraft that could have flown them here. A helicopter could have delivered them TO MY FRONT LAWN!"

My flash of temper seemed to shake him the rest of the way out of his stupor. "I'm the head of the Vice-Presidential detail, not the head of the Secret Service. I didn't make those decisions. Technically, now that you're the President, I'm just filling in to help out until the Presidential detail arrives."

"Half the Presidential detail is dead."

"I wasn't going to mention the possibility of promotion."

"So your colleague couldn't get the two men to stay together?"

"The Secretary was the priority."

"Where are the agent and the Secretary now?"

"The agent was ordered to remain on the plane and deliver the package. Otherwise we would have been placing the Secretary in the very same airport that the aide had disappeared in."

"Who's at the airport investigating the disappearance?"

"Men are en route."

I pulled my cell phone out and texted Sam to send military into the airport to assist with the Secret Service efforts. "Was Jared taken?" I asked George.

"No. They've already had airport security view the camera footage. He walked away."

This was a concept that was unfathomable to me. My mind wanted to reject what it was hearing. "He walked away?"

"Yes, Ma'am. He got a sandwich and a soda, started for the gate, paused for a second, turned into a store before reaching the gate, peeked back out, shook his head, turned around, and walked away. He was out of the airport and into one of the cabs lined up at the curb before anyone knew he was missing. Airport security is working on trying to get the license plate number off the back of the cab. They're sending the footage they have to the Secret Service now."

"I want it sent to the FBI and CIA, as well. Your fellow workers are proving to be incompetent. When what remains of the presidential detail does get here, no one else is taking it over from you. I don't care who walks through that door and says otherwise. No one's gone missing under your watch, yet."

"Yes, Ma'am."

"I'm going to ask you again, am I safe here?"

"You're safer here than if we tried to move you, for now."

I got a text back from Sam asking if it was Ronald, the head of the Secret Service, or me that was asking for the backup.

I snorted and texted back that I was ordering it because it seemed to me like Ronald was in over his head.

Sam texted right back, asking if I wanted a military takeover.

I told him, no. However, I did want the military to handle the transportation of our people in Colorado from now on. Moreover, I wanted somebody watching Ronald, really watching him.

All the while I texted with Sam, George texted his own messages.

"Have we started the screenings and tests with our people in Colorado, yet?" I asked George.

"Yes, Ma'am."

"Has Ronald been tested, yet?"

"He went first."

"I want the analysis on his test sent to me."

He showed no reaction to my order, just said, "Yes, Ma'am."

"Was Jared tested?"

"No, Ma'am."

"My orders were that everyone was to be tested before being transported back."

"He was on painkillers and they felt his tests wouldn't be accurate. The doctor had also given him pills to get him through his trip back. He's on our schedule to be tested tonight, after the last pill has time to wear off and before we clear him to come back into the building."

"What about the agent that was sent to watch him?"

"He was tested and passed without a hitch. Ma'am... at the risk of inciting your wrath, may I speak frankly?"

"Only if you're going to explain to me how in the hell this happened."

"I'm getting texts back that there were never orders given to provide aides with protection. Jared was only on the courtesy list."

"Courtesy list? After he'd already been a victim in the attack? Now you're just making stuff up."

He cracked his first smile. "Respectfully, Ma'am, we're here to protect the President, the first family, and the VP. Without a current VP, our protection now extends to the Speaker of the House, and given his condition, the Senate Pro Tempore. We have made moves to add the remaining members of the line of succession, given our unusual circumstances. Ronald asked you to issue that order so we could track them all, when everything first went down. But that's it, Ma'am. Courtesy protection is the idea that if an attack is made and we know you're secure, we'll then do all we can to save as many other employees and people as possible. We wouldn't just leave them to fend for themselves. However, we must maintain our priorities. Jared left the umbrella of protection when he walked off that plane. Ronald didn't do anything wrong, neither did the agent on the plane."

"And I still go back to the fact that they shouldn't have been on a commercial plane."

"We have a lot of people to move back and forth and they're all getting released from the hospital at different times. Some want to stay and wait for others, and others want to get back here as soon as they can. Agents offered Jared a secure flight back tonight, after all of today's discharges had been made. He didn't want to wait, and that was his choice. The Secretary of the Interior offered to fly with him so there'd be a modicum of protection extended to him."

"And now we have an aide, who has had more contact with the President than I did on most days, walk away from protection."

"Yes, Ma'am."

I thought for a moment, cocked my head to the side, and batted my eyelashes at him. "Tell me. Who has the President's cell phone?"

His eyes widened. "Jared does, Ma'am."

Will groaned.

"And I suppose it has now disappeared right along with him?" I asked.

"I'll text and see what the agent can figure out. Maybe it's in Jared's luggage," George offered.

I closed my eyes and sighed, letting a moment of insecurity show. "George..."

"It's not your fault, Ma'am. It's not the President's responsibility to extend the umbrella during a security crisis. It's only yours if you want to add specific individuals."

"Who was supposed to issue the order?"

"The Secretary of Homeland Security. He extends it by declaring a National Special Security Event."

"Which is why making up a list of individual people to protect wasn't on my checklist."

"Correct."

I breathed a sigh of relief. There had been a foul up, and I was plenty pissed about it, but it hadn't been my mistake. "And where is the Secretary of Homeland Security now?"

"He's back in the Situation Room."

"Thank you. Let me know when you have more news. I'm headed to the Sit Room."

"Yes, Ma'am."

I walked into the Sit Room ready to breathe fire. "Anthony!"

The Secretary of Homeland Security didn't say a word. He didn't move a muscle from his upright, but relaxed, posture in the chair.

"Anthony Gerald Montgomery!"

"I believe he's asleep, Ma'am," Sam said.

I considered throwing a clipboard at his head. I grabbed two metal domes off the buffet, instead. I walked over, stood behind the Secretary on my hit list, and clanged the domes together next to his head. *BANG! BANG! BANG!*

The man jumped up out of his seat and stood at attention.

People snickered.

"No one's playing Revelry," I told him. "Sit down and stop embarrassing yourself."

He sat and spun around in his chair to face me. "You rang?" he asked, his tone laced with dry humor.

If I hadn't been so pissed, I would have laughed. Instead, I fixed him with my best bitch-glare. I moved to replace the lids on the buffet and then walked to the head chair, waved everyone else into their chairs, and then chose to stand behind mine. I was determined to make all them look up at me from their seated positions. — I'd learned a thing or two about being a short woman commanding people in a man's world.

"Jared, the former President's personal assistant, is now missing. And it's my understanding that he didn't have Secret Service detail watching him because *somebody* didn't declare this mess a National Special Security Event." I looked at Anthony. "Do you have any idea who that person might be?"

The military trained man stood up to level the playing field. I couldn't blame him; I was calling him out in front of a captive audience.

"Ma'am, I have the declaration in my paperwork."

"Is it signed? Did you have a copy sent to Ronald?"

"Ma'am, I spoke to Henry and told him I was going to declare it. He told me, no, that I wasn't to do it."

"It wasn't his job to decide that, it was yours."

He looked me in the eye as he contemplated trying to argue that point. He sighed instead. "Yes, Ma'am."

"When did this little pow-wow take place?"

"Ma'am?"

"Did this conversation take place before or after I was sworn in?"

"There were two conversations. The first was just before the cabinet meeting. I told him I was going to declare it, and he asked me to wait. We had the meeting, you were sworn in, then he called me back saying not to do it."

"First of all, Will was here, in the building, as acting Chief of Staff in Henry's absence. Secondly, how would you know I would let Henry stay on in his position? There was a plan, but the plan got thrown out the window when everything went down."

He just looked at me, his face faltering.

"Jared is missing, Anthony. He's missing mainly because he didn't have a man assigned to him."

"Ma'am, I'm sorry."

"Why in the hell didn't you ask me about it when Henry countered what you instinctively wanted to do? Especially if you weren't confident enough to make the decision on your own, but still thought it should be done?"

"He gave me sound reason for holding off."

Henry cleared his throat.

My eyes shifted over to Henry before my head followed the movement. "Speak."

"When he called to tell me, I knew the Secret Service would be split bad enough as it was. I had Ronald telling me that they were going to extend themselves to cover the line of succession, and they were already short on men over there..." His eyes flashed over to Anthony and back. "I wasn't sure it would be in their best interests to spread themselves even thinner, trying to cover so many other people. So, I went around to the others in question and we took a vote to decline the protection."

I was somewhat mollified, now that somebody was saying something that made some sense. *Still though...* "I'm sure Jared voted to decline."

"Everyone voted to decline. We were in the hospital at the time, and the hospital was on lockdown because we had three of the cabinet members."

"Except then everyone started getting released and shipped back at different times. You should have made a change once that started happening. Jared wasn't taken, he walked off the grid at an airport mid-trip and we don't know why."

There was nothing Henry could say in response.

"And the fact of the matter is that the President was gone, I was next in line, yet you were still calling shots, and we hadn't even spoken yet. After I was sworn in, Will was the one here, the one I was talking to. And as such, you had no damned business telling someone here what to do. You had no confirmation from me personally that you were my go-to man."

"Ma'am, I'm sure you can understand that there was a bit of confusion going on at the time. We were all trying to reign in the chaos. I'm sorry if you feel I overstepped my bounds, I was doing what I thought best under the circumstances."

I angled myself so that I could address both Henry and Anthony. "I don't think that anyone in this room can argue that in order for the President to have been taken in as efficient a manner as possible, someone on the inside had to be feeding the enemy information."

They both gave a shake of their head.

"Didn't it occur to either one of you that Secret Service detail isn't only about protection of the individual, but there's also value to having the protected watched for odd behavior? Jared wouldn't have been able just to walk off, if eyes had been on him. Skilled eyes on him could have caught on to whatever he was up to."

They looked at each other, something passed between them, and then they looked back at me.

My skin crawled. I don't know why, but their shared look made me feel uncomfortable. Maybe they doubted me, maybe they knew I was right but were going to try to snowball me into dropping it so they could move on to what they felt were more important things... or maybe they were my traitors. Whatever it was, I didn't like it, not at all. "You're both excused."

Anthony blanched. "What?"

My mind flashed to the way Henry had come in here and dismissed me last night, which only furthered my resolve. "You two are hereby relieved of your duties."

"But you can't do that," Henry said.

"I believe that I just did. You serve at the pleasure of the President. I am the President, and I am displeased." I kept my eyes on them but turned my head in the direction of the door. "George!"

"Ma'am?" George asked as he entered from the hall.

"These two gentlemen have been relieved of their duties, and as such, should be removed from the premises," I said.

"Yes, Ma'am," George replied. Other agents had heard my voice from the hall and started to come in to escort the two men out.

Sam cleared his throat.

I made eye contact with him and already knew what he wanted. I wanted it too, just not inside this building. I nodded to him.

Sam called for his Marine guards that were outside in the hall, as well. "These two should be taken to the Pentagon for debriefing."

The agents stepped back and the guards removed the stunned men from the room.

I shivered with a chill. I seriously, seriously wanted a drink right now. I hadn't been drunk since that first campaign. I figured I was due.

"For the record," the Secretary of State said, "I would have done the same."

"As would I," Sam agreed.

I nodded. "Glad to know we're all on the same page." I let a moment pass in silence so we could finish letting our tired brains catch up with this latest happening. "It would please me if the two deputies would be willing to step up."

"Yes, Ma'am," Will said.

"Yes, Ma'am," Anthony's deputy said.

I turned to the deputy of Homeland Security. "Would you please sign that declaration and get the Secret Service the added backup they need?"

"Yes, Ma'am." He reached over to pick up the folder and get started.

I turned to the Attorney General, who'd taken to hanging around as much as possible, trying his best to keep us on the Constitutional path of righteousness. "Do whatever you have to do to make it so that these two can function without being questioned about their titles every time they try to do something."

"On it," he answered.

I turned to George, "The phone?"

"It's not in his carry on, and there were no checked bags. At this point we have to assume Jared still has Cartwright's cell."

"Well, isn't that just par for our course?" Sam said. "Why didn't the agent have it?"

"Jared has had it since the incident. It was thought that it would be fine, since Jared has had it off and on throughout the duration of his job as the President's personal aide. And with Jared accompanying the Secretary back, Ronald left it with him, thinking Jared could get it back to you sooner than his plan to put it on tonight's plane."

"I see. Ronald let Jared go without protection, and then he let the phone be entrusted to the unguarded man, to keep it safe."

"Do you think Jared has the ability to hack into it?"

"He can, if he's our traitor and he sends it to our captor friend, who forces Dad to get into it."

16 EENY, MEENY, MINY, MO — CATCH
A TRAITOR BY THE TOE

It felt like the dust from the employee overhaul was just beginning to settle in the room. I'd even picked at a few more bites to eat from the new plate in front of me.

We'd begun to kick around a few ideas for the next time our new friend made contact.

George gave one curt knock and burst back into the Sit Room with his phone to his ear. "Ma'am, Ronald has to speak to you. You're going to want to put him on speaker phone."

I nodded.

George had been acting as my point of contact, my representative of the Secret Service, because he was the highest-ranking man here. It gave me a face to talk to. But, apparently, we were beyond that with whatever Ronald needed to discuss.

Our tech guy took the phone and hooked it into a speaker system so that we'd all be sure to hear the head of Secret Service. A system could fade out any static and sharpen the sounds, as well as record the conversation for future review.

"All right, Ronald, you have everyone's attention," I announced, speaking a little louder than normal, for the sake of the speakerphone.

"Ma'am, we have a situation in the skies. The plane carrying the Secretary of the Interior is being rerouted and landed at Fort AP Hill, in Virginia."

I felt like banging my head on the tabletop, repeatedly. "Why?"

"There was an Oriental man, speaking broken English. Who, when he boarded, took his time walking through business class to coach. Then the man stalled a bit before taking his seat. He seemed to be trying to look around business class without appearing to actually be looking around. Once in flight, he kept getting up to use the bathroom. A stewardess questioned him, and he claimed that flying made him nervous, which caused him intestinal distress. This all caught the attention of our agent, who began watching him at this point. He also caught the attention of the two Air Marshals onboard."

"The flight had two Air Marshals?" I asked.

"The FAA upped security, due to the disappearance of the President. September eleventh still haunts them. We'd also made them aware of the agent and VIP passengers onboard. Our three guys were then given a courtesy flight in business class to get them back to DC. With everything that's going on, the airline decided to tighten their own security.

"So what move did the guy make to trip the final alarm?"

"After his third trip, the stewardess asked him to use the rear bathrooms in coach. He agreed, but then went back to the forward bathroom, in between the two classes for his fifth trip. He claimed those bathrooms were larger, which they aren't. Then he tried to claim an aisle seat closer to the bathrooms, saying he was worried about not making it in time, all the while he was stealing glances at our missing aide's seat. Nods were exchanged between the agent and Air Marshals, and now the man is being held in a seat, in the back row, at gunpoint."

"Broken English you said, where's he from?"

"Passport says Canada, but Canada says it's stolen. Says the owner of the passport looks very similar to the passenger, but authorities found the owner's body in his home, early this morning. The Coroner report estimates that the man has been dead for two days. The passport was fine through scanning at airport check-in because the authorities hadn't processed the paperwork on the death yet. The discovery of the body was still too new at that point. Because the death looked suspicious, they ran the victim's name through the system, and the hit on the passport came up shortly before the Air Marshals reported the disturbance to the pilot."

"Is the guy at least speaking French?"

"No, Ma'am. He's speaking a form of Japanese. A civilian onboard offered to translate when the man began babbling on and on about his innocence of any wrongdoing, his need to use the restroom, and his need of medication for his problem that he left in his checked baggage."

"And I'm guessing that they haven't let him go back into the bathroom, and that he hasn't soiled himself."

"You would be correct."

"A form of Japanese, explain that."

"Our agent recorded some of his ramblings and sent them for a regional identification, when the civilian said the suspect kept mixing dialectal words. Some she recognized, others she didn't. Language analysis says the mix of words and nuances of the accent he's using don't match up completely with any known dialect. He could have moved from one region of the country to another while being raised, but it's more likely that he's faking it altogether. And none of it explains why he had a dead Canadian's passport."

I looked over at Sam. "Fort Hill is a training base, right?"

"Yes, Ma'am. It's an Army base, but we train different branches of our military to work together there."

"Perfect," I said. "Ronald, this guy isn't going to give us anything easily. Let's wear him out by letting trainee, after trainee, after trainee, practice their interrogation skills on him. Our people have to be itching for some sort of action other than holding their breath and waiting for orders. We'll go ahead and give them a little toy to play with."

Sam smirked and nodded his approval.

"How are the remaining passengers getting to their destination?" I asked.

"Once they land, the passengers will be quickly questioned, and the plane will be given a safety inspection and total sweep. The Air Marshalls and the remaining passengers will then be allowed to take off and complete their flight to DC. The agent and the Secretary will be given a military helicopter ride into town," Ronald reported.

"Is there any other support that you need?" I asked.

"No, thank you. I have military backup now. The most helpful thing everyone can do is to gather in as few a number of places as possible, so we don't have to spread ourselves out so far. Now that I have the umbrella extended, I have the authority to make people wait until we can fly them in groups.... Ma'am, when I didn't get the declaration, I assumed —"

"It's fine, you're fine. At this point, I only question why the President's phone was given to a non-agent."

Ronald gave me his I'm-going-to-level-with-you sigh. "Who am I supposed to trust? I'd like to think I can trust all my people, but can I? If I gave it to the agent and he ended up being our traitor, what then? I let Jared keep it because that man has been trusted with the President's phone for six years. It felt safer than giving it to a man who has never has the privilege of being trusted with it before. I also figured there couldn't be much on that phone that Jared wasn't already privy to. I had wanted to deliver it to you myself, but I'm tied up here and you wanted it now."

"All right."

"I'm sorry, Mr. Secretary of Defense, I just want to be clear," Ronald went on to say. "You'll send orders for your guys to take custody of our suspect, releasing the Secret Service of the responsibility?"

Sam looked at me before answering.

I nodded to him, thinking the military trainees might actually be more trustworthy right now.

"Yes, Ronald," Sam answered. "Everything will be on file. They'll have papers to hand the agent, and both Marshalls, so they are confident that they are legally releasing custody."

"Anything else, Ronald?" I asked.

"No, Ma'am, thank you."

"Thank you," I said and gave the signal for the tech to disconnect the call. I looked around the room at all the thoughtful faces. "So... what's up with our supposedly incontinent, non-fluent Japanese speaking, Canadian imposter friend?"

"I'd like to venture a guess," Sam said.

"The floor is yours."

"Our captor threatened to come after you. I think we can agree that would be a difficult feat, given the level of security around you now and the fact that you haven't left the building since this started, and he seems to be a small operation. Realizing this, he probably sent someone to watch the hospital and go after anyone he could. Maybe he only seemed interested in the empty seat and was really eyeing up the accessibility of the Secretary. Or, maybe, Jared is our traitor and they were setting it up to look like he was the next victim and their wires got crossed. Maybe they were confused on the location they were to stage a kidnapping, to make it look like the enemy had snagged a second guy when really they were just retrieving Jared."

"So, we really think the fake Canadian is definitely connected to the kidnappers, not someone else with poor timing?"

"We assume he's connected. If we're right, he's going to hide behind not being a citizen and not knowing the governmental issues we're going through, despite it being international news. He's going to deny even being in the vicinity of a television or newspaper, so he can hide behind a veil of ignorance, especially as he pretends not to be able to speak our language. We're going to wear him down until we get something out of him. He's holding a dead Canadian's passport, and he just happens to be on the same plane as federal staff? That man is guilty of something and it's not uncontrollable defecation. And when we're done with him, Canada is going to get a turn."

"Ma'am?" the director of the FBI said, looking up from his laptop screen. "If I can have a moment of your attention?"

"It's yours."

"There was a hit, seven minutes ago, on Jared's personal credit card. He rented a car. The owner of the company is reporting that Jared came onsite in a cab, paid the driver, and came inside, asking to rent whatever the owner had available. He signed an agreement, the card was swiped, the keys were handed over, and he left."

"No one had put a hold on his cards so they would trip an alarm and the charge couldn't be put through?"

"No, Ma'am. There's a hold on his White House charge because he fell off the grid. We can't put a hold on his personal finances. He technically hasn't been found guilty of doing anything wrong, yet. In theory, he could just be devising another way to get here with the President's phone, which is an item that he was personally entrusted with."

"So then how did you get the info?"

"Because he is now a suspect, and because he does hold a valued item, we put a tracer on his cards. Instead of holding him up at some civilian's counter, possibly putting innocent lives at risk, if he decided to set up a hostage situation while waiting for us to get there, or have him harm the desk clerk in order to steal the keys, we used his card to trace his purchases. Now we're using the GPS tracker on the car to trace his movements. We can follow him again. He just put himself back on the grid."

Hope flared in my heart, because I liked Jared. I didn't want him to be our traitor. "Does he know he's back on the grid? Did he do it on purpose?"

"We don't know. What we do know is that he hasn't made a call with either his White House phone, or his personal cell. If he wanted back on the grid, why wouldn't he call in and ask for help?"

"Was he still by himself?"

"Yes."

"So now we wait?" I asked, frustration tingeing my voice because I was about done with the whole waiting thing.

"Yes, we'll get people into position, keep a reasonable pillow around him to make him think we aren't on to him, and hope he's stupid enough to lead us somewhere important."

"He's got to know that we'll find a way to get to him," Will said.

"He might be panicked and hiding behind a false sense of security," the director replied.

"He's not going to fall for this. He's been hanging around all of us for too long," I said.

"I'm sorry, Ma'am. It's all we've got at the moment," the director said.

"I'm just saying, make damned sure he's not leading your men into a trap. He may not even be meeting anyone. If he's a part of this mess, he could just be driving in a direction away from where our attention needs to be." *Great, now I was starting to sound like Sam.*

"We're on it."

"Meanwhile, he has Dad's phone."

Sam spoke, "He can't get into that phone. If there's anything of importance on it, that he doesn't want someone to see, then he's already destroyed it. You need to give up on the phone."

"Not unless Jared is going to send it to wherever Dad is," I muttered. *Ugh!* I needed a timeout. "Okay, so if the airplane guy was the captor's attempt at a power play, and it failed, we're probably not going to hear or see from him until he regroups, right?"

"Probably," Sam answered.

"And Jared is going to need time to drive to wherever it is he's going?"

"We would assume so."

"All right, my head needs a mental break to process. Would this, or would this not, be a good time for me to go lay down?"

Everyone nodded, which I took as a general consensus that I could go.

Will went to the main door and asked George to accompany me inside the office, because there were a few things he needed to deal with. Now that he officially had the elevated responsibilities of Chief of Staff, he felt the need to be in the Sit Room when I wasn't. But he also knew I didn't want to be left alone, if it could be helped.

George followed me into the private study and positioned himself in the corner by the door. Him and I functioning independently of each other, while occupying the same space, was nothing new. The corner was a position he had taken up a thousand times before, when security was tight and I was in a less secure location than I was now. It's just that this time he had his face buried in a tablet, as information was passed back and forth between him and other agents.

I used the bathroom quickly, not wanting to break my human security blanket for longer that I had to, and knowing George wasn't about to follow me in here unless I fell or something.

Then I lay down on the couch, facing the back cushions. I covered myself with a blanket, and tried to relax. I was trying to let the stress go so I could get my head to stop spinning with all the possible betrayals we were facing.

Scenes from the day kept replaying in my brain. I'd close my eyes, and there they'd be. The description of the footage of Jared walking away — *I really should have that footage streamed into the Sit Room so we could view it.* The creepy feeling I got when Henry and Anthony had shared that look. The picture in my head of that flight and the horror the citizens must be feeling in knowing there was a suspected terrorist on the plane. The moment of insecurity I'd felt, wondering if traitors in my midst were guiding me to suspect the wrong people.

Then there was the heartache of knowing that somewhere on this planet, my father existed, in pain, staring his own doom in the face, and wondering how much longer it would go on before ending. Then followed the torture of my brain telling me there was nothing I could do to stop the inevitable from happening.

I tried to picture us locating them, and Special Forces going in to get them. Then the cold knowledge would settle in that the sole focus of the captor, upon hearing them come after him, would be to aim a gun at Dad and kill him before he turned the gun on himself, so we couldn't hold him in prison for the rest of his life.

My mind tried to salvage the situation. It went to a bright, happy image of my father reuniting with my mother and brother. Then utter despair consumed me as the vision clouded over and they all faded, leaving me behind to survive alone, without even just one of them to hold onto this time.

At some point in my mind's wonderings, I'd begun to cry into my pillow. The crying had turned into sobs. And the sobs had prompted George, who'd never witnessed my tears before, to sit me up and hold me in an awkward hug.

The hug wasn't helping. I just felt even worse because George had felt bad enough to attempt to physically comfort me. My sobs turned to blubbering because I was trying to apologize to him, not that he could understand me.

Will had entered the outer office to make some calls in a never-ending effort to keep the country functioning in the midst of all this mess. I had gotten so loud, and his ears so attuned to me, that he had heard me through the door.

Will came in, and George turned to give him a, beyond relieved, look of appreciation. George was fully aware of the personal relationship Will and I shared, and felt that was reason enough to turn me over to him. Will stepped forward, without any prompting, to claim me, and George disengaged his arms as he gently transferred me into Will's.

Will pulled me up into a standing position and wrapped his arms around me. He knew I'd calm down if he just stood there, his arms feeling all safe, solid, and stronger than I thought I was.

"It's," *sob,* "not," *hitched breath,* "weakness," I said, hoping George would understand me this time. "It's," *sob,* "stress," *sniffle,* "release," *snort,* "for girls," *soft wail.*

"Oh, I know. I grew up with two sisters. They were never meaner or able to kick harder than when they were about to ball, or were already balling, their eyes out. You go ahead and work it out, I'll be waiting the on the other side of the door."

Will let me cry it out and then got me settled on the couch and covered back up. He sat on the floor, one hand rubbing my shoulders, the other texting staff members, until I finally drifted into the oblivion of exhausted, dreamless sleep. *Hallelujah.*

He'd then stepped back into the office, and George came back into the corner of the study to stand guard.

17 JARED, THE FAKE CANADIAN, AND FEDERAL EXPRESS

I slept for all of about two hours before I was woken up.

"Ma'am, the Director of the FBI wants to talk to you as soon as you're able," George said in a soft, yet firm, voice.

The immediate past came rushing back into the forefront of my mind in one felled swoop.

It reminded me of those first few days after Mom and Jacob had died. How I'd forget about what had happened while I was asleep, only to wake up and have to remember it all over again. I'd had a love/hate relationship with sleep for quite a while. I loved the relief of the oblivion, but hated the fresh horror of waking up.

And here it was starting all over again, the cycle from hell.

There was no snooze-button option like the one I'd cared for and protected my right to, upstairs, next to my comfy bed. The cold reality was enough to shock my system awake. The more I woke up, the more I registered feeling chilly, which was only made worse when I tossed the blanket aside and sat up. *No doubt a symptom from my overall lack of sleep.*

I was cold, shivering, and my chattering teeth felt grimy. "Can you send someone up to the residence to grab me a sweater, and a cup of coffee? Please?" I asked George.

"I'll text Nikki for you," he replied.

I closed my eyes at my own stupidity. "Oh, crap. I could have done that."

He chuckled; this wasn't the first time he'd seen me try to wake up in a hurry. "It's no problem."

I headed for the bathroom and paused in front of the mirror long enough to gather my flyaway hair into a bun, and swipe a supplied toothbrush over my teeth. Someday, I'd really have to remember to take the time to floss again.

I was still a little bleary-eyed when I walked into the Sit Room. There was already a sweater from my VP office and a cup of coffee waiting for me. I grabbed the sweater off the back of my chair, pulled it on, and flopped down in the seat. I settled my gaze on the FBI Director, "What do you have for me?"

"Jared made a stop at a Fed-Ex shipping center," he announced.

The last of my sleep-fog cleared from my brain as I sat up a little straighter. "You have my undivided attention."

"We tracked the stop twenty minutes ago. He was there for seven minutes and left. Our guys walked in three minutes later, to find the clerk looking at the package with a frown on her face and the number for the local FBI office nearly dialed into the telephone."

I looked around at the others in the room. I realized that they had already been told this much while they were waiting for me. Now their eyes and ears focused on the director, ready to hear the rest of the story. "We're all waiting with baited breath."

"It seems Jared had walked in and asked the attendant to box up a sealed cell phone. Then he addressed the package to the White House, in care of you. He flashed his White House ID and paid on his personal credit card to have it shipped by the quickest method possible. Then he left. In light of recent happenings, the attendant didn't want to take the chance and put delivery through. She had pulled up the number for the local Bureau office to try to turn it over to us. She was afraid that it was some sort of explosive, yet was just as afraid that it was something you needed. She readily turned it over to our people. It appeared to be the Presidential phone, intact, and unaltered. They'll scan it before bringing it in here, just to make sure it's nothing more than a phone."

"What is he doing?" I asked.

"Jared? He seemed agitated and nervous. He was in a hurry to get back on the road."

I rubbed my forehead. "He's been driving for a few hours now. Is he headed in a general direction?"

"Well, it's a bit of a snaking route, but we have an idea. We think he may be headed to Camp David."

I sat back in my chair and gave a slightly relieved sigh. "He knows Camp David is going to be guarded."

"Ma'am?"

"He's running scared."

"Well, he's not running smart."

"He hasn't been trained to run smart, he's been trained to run the President's errands."

"Maybe he's been trained by someone else," the Director muttered. "What errand do you think he could be running now?"

"He's insuring the package gets delivered," I answered.

"But did he intend for it to get to us, or was he just putting up a show while expecting someone else to go inside the building, after he left, to forcefully reclaim the package?"

I cocked an eyebrow. "Your boys can't answer that one?"

"The priority was to get their hands on whatever he was sending. The attendant was given a panic button to hit if anyone else comes in wanting that package. Meanwhile, we'll keep a surveillance team nearby in case they do. But if someone saw our boys in there and turned away... there's no way to know that. Besides, if he knows Camp David is guarded, and he's headed there, why wouldn't he just hold onto it and turn the phone over when he gets there?"

"Okay, so why else would he head for Camp David?"

"I don't know, but it's just a direction, not a known destination. Camp David is in the middle of the forest. Maybe they have a spot nearby."

"Tell me, what you know for certain, about what he's doing."

"He knows he's being followed, that's why he's taking a serpentine route. He's not speeding, so he's not trying to outrun anybody, but he's not wasting any time."

"Does he know it's us following him?"

"We haven't identified ourselves."

I drummed my fingers on my bottom lip, thinking. "I feel like we're making him our easy scapegoat. We're so desperate to point a finger, and he's gone and made himself stand out."

"No one has assumed it's him. And no one is assuming that if it is him, he's the only one."

"Is it possible that he fears our enemy is following him? Could that be why he separated the phone from himself and sent it to me? Thinking he could lure our enemies away from the phone?"

"He'd have to think they were after the phone. He'd have to know there was something worthwhile on it."

"Or, he could have already been convinced there was, by my wanting it so damned bad. He knows I want it because it might hold a clue. If he thinks the enemy is following him, he may be thinking it's a matter of time before they make their move. Send the phone to me so at least they don't get that, head in the direction of DC, and wait for fate to play out. He could be detouring to Camp David to keep the drama out of DC, which would only draw public attention to another missing person. He could be convinced that the enemy might be picking him to strike against next and be stalling for time."

"Then why wouldn't he have just gotten back on the damned plane to begin with?"

"That is the million-dollar question, isn't it? Something's been bugging me since you gave me the description of his behavior at the gate. Show me the footage from airport security. Put it up on my magic screens."

The Director gestured at the tech guy, who nodded and started hitting buttons.

"If he's scared that he's being followed by the enemy," Sam asked, "then why not call somebody?"

"One, he knew that he wasn't under Secret Service protection, because he voted against it. Two, he knows walking away makes him a suspect, and maybe he doesn't think it's safe to call in. And three, the twenty-six-year-old, lovable idiot thinks he might be saving the world by leading them on a wild goose chase because he no longer has the phone."

"If he's innocent," our new Secretary of Homeland Security said, "he is an idiot. If he's a traitor, then he's pure genius. We're all sitting here, watching him, analyzing him, spinning our wheels while waiting to see his next move, and he's driving around, leading a merry chase, while something equally duplicitous is happening elsewhere."

The footage began playing on the front wall. We all watched as the scene, larger than life, unfolded in the airport. It was enhanced as the figures moved across the screen. Jared and our Japanese fake-Canadian had remained untouched as the rest of the scene was dimmed, in order to highlight our two suspects.

"You can't see Jared's face when he looks towards the gate. Can anyone get me an angle off another camera that shows his face?" I asked.

The FBI Director started clicking and typing. "I'm getting people on it."

"I want a couple of your profilers to read his body language when he first looks and then freezes, when he peaks around the wall from the store, and then when he shakes his head and walks away."

"Yes, Ma'am."

"If you can get an angle on his face and body language from the front, you send that to your profilers, too. I want a definitive answer on whether Jared is a traitor."

"Yes, Ma'am."

"If he is our traitor, awesome, at least now he's no longer on the inside. If he isn't, then we need to stop being preoccupied with him and figure out who it really is."

"Even if he is a traitor, it doesn't mean he's the only one."

"Understood, but at least I'd feel like we were making progress." I shook off the topic of Jared and took a mental roll call of those present in the room. We all seemed to be taking turns drifting in and out, as we took care of other things or tried to grab a few hours rest before the next onslaught hit.

"Any word yet from our resurrected Canadian?" I asked Sam.

"Well, his Japanese is worse than his English, but that doesn't stop him from pretending not to speak English. We've pointed out to him that he was speaking English to the stewardess on the plane. He claims he only learned enough phrases to explain his anxiety problems."

I rolled my eyes and shook my head. "He's stupider than Jared is, if he thinks we're going to buy into that nonsense... Was there even any medication in his checked baggage?"

"There was no checked baggage."

"I bet he claims the airline must have lost it."

"Of course, he does, and he just happened to lose his claim tickets as well. Never mind the fact that there were no claim tickets issued in association with his boarding pass."

"So what language does he actually speak with some sort of proficiency?"

"The trainees are working on it. The likely plan is that he'll eventually become so agitated over having one team, after another, after another come in to question him that he'll eventually just give himself up to make the parade stop."

"None of the trainees are showing any promise?"

"All the trainees are watching a live feed of the questionings. There are two trainees of South Korean descent in the audience. They both believe that this man looks much more Korean than he does Japanese. And while, as we know, looks can be very deceiving in trying to determine citizenship, they're concocting a plan to figure out if it can help us this time."

"How much longer are they going to take to concoct it?"

"They're consulting with their trainers. Right now, those two have the best plan. They're only going to get one shot at it, so they're trying to cover their bases."

"I'm really, really getting impatient with all of this."

"Would you approve a full-on interrogation?"

I started squeezing my head between my hands again and sighed. "What would you do?"

"Interrogations go smoother if we're yelling and screaming in the language of fluency and we know the culture the individual was raised in. Give the twosome a shot. A little information can go a long way in knowing what buttons to push to interrogate with. Then we can send in the professionals.

"Besides," he continued, "he had no weapons, nothing on him to make himself look particularly malicious. It'd be very hard to prove cause, if an interrogation leaked out and the press demanded to know why we treated him that way. I mean, under the circumstances, we'll do what needs to be done, it'd just be nice to pave the way a little, if the trainees could get something out of him."

I chose to ignore the fact that he hadn't actually answered my question. "Is the guy built?"

"He's got muscle." He signaled the tech guy, who hit a button, and a picture of the guy appeared on the screen.

"You got live footage of him in custody?"

Sam gave a head-nod and video footage appeared. We listened as a group of three trainees took their shot at him. "This is a live feed. Those three men represent Army, Navy, and Marines. They've been in the service for at least fifteen years apiece. They're at the fort to train on how to share information between the branches so that each branch's strengths can be used to compensate for the other branches' areas of weakness. They volunteered for this challenge and have been collaborating together."

"It doesn't look like it's working," I commented as I watched the suspect sit there in silence, his alert eyes staring at a fixed point on the wall, the corner of his mouth turned up, his posture relaxed.

"No, but they might have been more effective in a different setting. Instead, to our airplane friend, they're just the next Larry, Mo, and Curly to show up in front of him."

I thought about the comment that was made earlier about the guy not having any weapons with him on the plane. I took in his lean, muscular build and the way he held himself in the chair. "Our Canadian imposter doesn't need any weapons."

"I know."

"He's just playing possum."

"I know."

I chuckled as I continued to look him over. "He's all hard muscle and bemused patience. All he's doing is looking for a moment to retaliate, and then limbs will start flying and soldiers will be eating linoleum."

"I know."

"You know he smells like a martial arts bomb nearing the explosion point?"

"Yep. The profilers confirmed it."

That must be why he wanted to be able to pave the way of explanation for the press. He knew any real attempts at interrogation were going to get ugly with this guy. "And?"

"And, I want our Korean duo to finish planning and get their chance at him."

I raised an eyebrow of interest at the tone he'd used and felt the corners of my mouth turn up. "I want to watch a live feed of that."

Sam almost smiled at me. "I'll make the popcorn."

I didn't want to voice my fear of exactly where our man of mystery hailed from. The thought of it made my stomach clench. The more I looked up at the image of the guy, the more I worried we were walking straight towards a nuclear war.

"Is it time to start expecting contact again?" I asked.

"Only if he's figured out we have his guy. There may not have been a plan, only an order to find an opening to snag someone and go for it."

"Wouldn't the dude be late in touching base by now?"

He shrugged. "He had no phone or technology on him, which is suspicious in and of itself. I don't know if he was supposed to make contact, or simply show up somewhere when he had a hostage. Our apparent mastermind may very well have wanted to limit any communications between them because he'd know we'd be monitoring any foreign calls being pinged off any of our satellites."

"So how is he supposed to know if something happened to spoil the plans?"

"He won't. He probably wasn't counting on snagging another, or he has others out there, watching and waiting. Meanwhile, he's probably watching our news channels, and waiting to see if they show anything. Those news channels might be their only source of real communication at this point."

"So, the guy we saw on camera with Dad probably isn't the one who snagged him?"

"It's hard to say. He was taken by the survivors from the team that attacked. Judging from the way it looks like they made off with him in a floatplane, I'd say only two from the team escorted him away. Witnesses say this guy doesn't look familiar, but maybe he was left to guard and pilot the plane while the others were hired to handle the attack."

"Still no word on what happened to the plane's original pilot and instructor?"

"Nope. And their pictures and descriptions don't match anything the witnesses saw."

"Your guess?"

"My guess is that the attackers took the bodies and made them disappear. We've done searches and investigations of both of their houses and spoken with their families. There's nothing there to make us suspect either one had anything to do with it. The stories that the small airport reported to us both check out. They appear to be exactly who they said they were."

"How do you steal a plane in mid-air?"

"You can steal anything from anywhere, if you have the skills and you want it bad enough."

Yeah, tell me about it, I thought as I snorted at his comment.

18 A GHOST, A PHONE CALL, AND A BOTTLE OF PILLS

I was up in the Oval, watching the sun rise while listening to representatives from China tell me, over the phone, about how they swear they weren't in on the kidnapping. They extended their offer of help, and said they would like to be on the list of phone calls made the minute we find out who was behind this. They also assured me that if the captor and his cohorts are found to be on their soil, I had their offer of going in to round up the group for us. They didn't want people who could do this kind of thing on their own to be on Chinese soil. — Which was code for them not wanting the same thing to happen to their government.

I told them that, should it turn out that the perpetrators were within their boundaries, I would love it if our boys could join forces with theirs and go in to gather them up together. However, something in my gut told me theirs was not the country harboring my targets.

Then I heard the telltale sound of chopper blades closing in on the building and excused myself from continuing the conversation.

I was just grateful to be able to stop with the politically charged, yet must always be polite and correct no matter what, banter that one must have skills in when men in suits stood and arm-wrestled each other with words. I had more of a reputation for cutting to the chase, but I was female and amusing then and not, you know, actually the President. This was pretty much why I had been content to keep the Secretary of State busy handling the banter with other countries.

"Nikki!" I called out as I adjusted the position of the phone on the desktop and picked up my water bottle. — I still wasn't past the point of keeping the office the exact same way Dad had kept it. I might be using the office space, but it still didn't feel like it was mine yet.

"Ma'am?" Nikki said upon entering.

"Grab a guy from forensics hanging around the building and take him up to the Lincoln bedroom. Have him grab some stuff out of the bottom drawer of Dad's nightstand that he thinks he can lift some prints from. Then grab my contact bag out of my bathroom closet. Bring the guy and the bag down to the Sit Room."

"Um..." the look on her face was stark terror mixed with an annoyance in knowing I could see the fear in her eyes.

"Oh, come on. Dad slept in that room every night and only claims to have seen him once."

"Isn't there anything in here, or the private study, that might have his prints on them?"

"Everything in here gets wiped down every single day, pens, paperclips, and all. The stuff in the study is either cleaned or handled by other people, like Charlotte, before it's handed to him."

"Oh, Charlotte! I'll have Charlotte take someone up, with your permission."

I rolled my eyes. "Fine. Tell her that if Lincoln should happen to appear, I'd like for him to break his silence and give me a little advice."

She looked stricken. "If she comes back down those stairs with a message, I quit."

I laughed at her as she walked out. I took a different door out to the hallway and hit a button on the elevator. It opened a moment later as Will came up behind me, holding the long-awaited cell phone. He and I got on the elevator to go down.

"The Speaker of the House called," Will said. "He's going to survive, but has been vehemently advised to resign and retire."

I groaned, loud. "I'm going to have to appoint a VP as soon as possible. There's no way in Hell I'm going to let Congress elect their own Speaker with the thought in mind of planting someone in the White House, all the while waiting until I crack and run away for good, so their new man can swoop in. I know who they'll pick, too. Forget about checks and balances, both the branches will have the same agenda and they'll have a field day. The Supreme Court will spend their days, in their branch, trying to keep the other two in check.

"Who do you want?"

"I can't appoint anybody before Dad is officially gone. While being practical, it would be bad form before the permanency of my new title is set in stone."

"You should still give me a short list of names. I can have people start looking at FBI files, and begin running some preliminary interviews. Once he's gone, you'll want to move fast."

The elevator doors opened and we crossed through the hall to enter the

Sit Room. When we walked in, Will held up the phone.

The tech guy's eyes lit up. "Are you sure you can get into it, Ma'am? Because if it senses a hacking, programs and records will self-destruct, including the text conversations."

"I'm reasonably certain I can fake my way in. If I cause it to delete, then we're no worse off than if I hadn't tried at all."

"Have you had cause to fake it before?" Will asked.

I smiled. "Not since before that first campaign trail."

"Good to know," he said with a wink, totally making me think about the double entendre of a question like that coming from him.

I grinned like a little girl. The man was good for my blood pressure. For a few seconds, he'd made life feel normal again.

I held out my hand and he gave me the phone.

I tapped the screen twice and it lit up. I did the finger-slide thing to let it know I was serious about wanting it to wake, and it showed the screen for the password entry and the keyboard.

"The Presidential password has to have letters, numbers, a capital letter, at least one symbol, and be eight to ten characters in length," the tech guy said, reading off a punch list on his computer screen.

I closed my eyes and pictured Dad getting into his phone. The tap, the slide, and then the thumb would move very simply over the keyboard. Quick and efficient, nothing that would require a lot of memory or concentration on inputting — not with doing it a hundred times a day. And no way could he come up with a password that actually meant something to him, not with all those requirements...

The keyboard was set up for the first letter to be a capital, as though it planned on you starting a sentence... *Letters, numbers, symbols*... Whenever Dad had absently tapped his pen on a tabletop, he'd always tapped it in sets of three. We used to laugh about it. *Eight to ten characters*... Nine had three sets of three in it.

Quick, efficient, thumb taps... I'd had a strategy for this password thing. I'd just needed to know what his keyboard looked like. I knew that they periodically asked us all to change our passwords, and Dad had changed the keyboard he used on his phone just as often. I knew the key to his password would lie in the setup of his keyboard. Now all I needed to figure out was what pattern of buttons he used when tapping in the password.

Since the keyboard was set up for the first letter to be a capital, I figured he went with letters fist. I tapped in *Q w e*. Then I touched the number pad key. *Hmmm,* along the top row were five symbol keys, before the numbers started. I touched the first three buttons, *# $ &*, skipped the next two symbol keys, then *1 2 3*.

Bingo. The screen changed, waiting for a thumbprint.

I held the phone up for everyone to see. I'm not gonna lie, the teenager buried inside me felt highly accomplished at cracking a parental code with such ease.

Charlotte and the forensics guy walked in. He was wearing gloves and carrying a couple items that should hold the key to cracking step two in my little hacking venture.

"Ma'am," Charlotte said, "he said a house divided cannot stand. Find the traitors and execute them."

My jaw dropped open and my eyes all but popped out of my head.

"I'm kidding."

I started breathing again. "You have never, ever kidded with me before. I don't know if my heart can take it."

Will didn't know what the joke was based on, but he started chuckling at my reaction to it, nonetheless.

"I'm a hoot and a half, once I get started." She handed me my contact bag. "Do you need anything else from me? If not, I have need to speak to Nikki," she said with a wink.

"You will come clean before she actually leaves the building, right?"

"I'll try."

I laughed. "Go, thank you."

"You're welcome, Madam President."

I looked at the forensics guy. "Use some tape or something and lift a thumbprint off the Cheetos bag and transfer it into this phone for me, would you?"

He hesitated before accepting the phone from my hand. "...Ma'am?"

"Pretty please," and I added a sweet smile.

"But..." he looked over to Sam for help, "I can't help you hack into the President's phone."

"But I'm the president, and this is not my phone. Therefore, this is no longer the President's phone. So, you can help me do this."

"It's okay," Sam said. "That phone now belongs to the former President and we have to debrief and wipe his technology. There's no crime. We're just following protocol. We would have to do this if the President had suddenly become too ill to finish serving and couldn't open it himself."

The guy from forensics turned back to me and handed the phone back. "I have to see if I can borrow a kit off Secret Service. I didn't know what you were going to want me to do ahead of time, I'm unprepared for this."

"George is outside the door. I'm sure they keep a kit here, somewhere."

He nodded. "They do. I'll be right back."

"Ma'am." The Director of the FBI head-nodded towards the front wall.

Footage of Jared in the airport appeared. We had a front view of his face this time. We watched as he froze, and then we watched as he ducked into the store and peeked around the wall. We then had a side-view of his face when he paused again, and shook his head. Then there was a front view when he walked away and headed for the escalator to the ground floor.

"It looked as though he saw something he didn't like," I said. "Do you think he spotted the guy we have in custody?"

"The profilers said he went from uneasy, to confused, to fearful, then back to uneasy. Our unknown subject was there, getting on the plane, but he showed no signs of recognizing the man. We're not certain that Jared even spotted him," the Director said.

"So, where do we stand on him then?"

"I think we should make contact. Find out for sure if we're dealing with a suspect or just a person of interest."

"Agreed." I reached into my pocket and came up empty-handed. I looked around the room, "Someone find me my phone so I can call him."

Will gave a nod and started tapping on his phone.

"Ma'am, I understand if you want to make the call yourself. But you should do it on a White House phone," the Director told me.

"My cell is a White House phone."

"It should be from a landline."

"He won't know who is calling him then. But he'll recognize my cell number."

"Ma'am?" Will questioned.

I was starting to get tired of having to explain my every move. I knew that I had told them to question me, to make sure I wasn't acting out of emotion, but it still took all I had not to snap at them. "I talk to him all the time about my father. Dad didn't have a first lady to make sure he was eating and getting exercise, or if he had forgotten to take care of something. So, I did it. I called in to Jared and spoke with him almost every day. If he doesn't answer for me, he's not going to answer for anybody."

"I understand," the Director said, "but a landline would be easier for us to track and record."

I shook my head, determined to remain stubborn on this one. "No. Hook it up to one of those black boxes you people have, and track it that way. If he's running scared, I want him to know I'm throwing him a lifeline. Besides, you know where he is. And the box thingy will record it so you can amplify sound and voice intonations and all that stuff when you play it back."

The Director signaled for the tech guy to indulge me and the tech guy picked up his phone. I assumed he was calling and requesting someone to bring in a box thing.

The forensics dude came back into the room and settled himself in a corner to work on lifting a few thumbprints.

Nikki came in next. She crossed the room, and on her way by, plucked the contact bag out of the crook of my arm. She disappeared into the office for a few moments and returned with my phone. "Under your pillow,

Ma'am."

She'd laced her tone with sarcasm, but somehow tagging the 'Ma'am' onto the end of her comment had made it seem less terse. Maybe that was why people were always saying 'sir' and 'ma'am' around here. It was code for, 'I'm going to tell you exactly what I think, but you can't get mad because I showed respect for your title.'

"Well, that's a new place," I said.

She smirked. "If you say so, Ma'am."

"Issue?"

She stopped and sighed. "A broken heel. It seems to have snapped off when I all but jumped out of my skin when Charlotte stopped to talk to me."

I started laughing. "Go up to my room and get a pair of my shoes to wear."

"No, thank you, Ma'am, I'll manage. I now prefer to not enter the residence, at all." She turned and left the room.

I looked over at Will. "Do you think that if I issued an Executive Order, I could get people to stop calling me 'Ma'am' at the beginning and end of every conversation? Could I get them to remove it from everyone's vocabulary?"

He smirked and nodded. "Sure, they can switch to Madam President, President Cartwright, President Cartwright the Second, President Cartwright the Sequel, or President Cartwright Take Two. My vote is for the latter. It's just that 'Ma'am' is shorter."

"Whatever."

"Yes, Ma'am."

Half-chuckles and grins circled around me.

One of the aides came in with a black plastic box and carried it over to the tech guy, before excusing himself right back out of the room. The tech guy stood and brought the box over to get my phone and set up the device. When he was done, he handed the phone back to me and gave me a nod to go ahead and make the call to Jared.

George had followed the aide in and was standing by the door, on the inside now, to hear what we were about to find out.

I sat on the edge of the massive table and assumed a relaxed posture, hoping that would help me make my voice sound casual as well. I pulled up my list of contacts and hit the button to dial his cell phone.

It rang once, twice, three times, before he finally answered, but didn't speak.

"Honey... Sweetie... Sugar Pie, Apple Dumpling, Honey Bunch —" I said in a sweet voice.

I finally heard a big sigh of relief. "I don't know what to do! Tell me what to do!" Jared pleaded.

I almost smiled. "Tell me what happened. Why did you get off the plane?"

"I swear to God, Molly, I was hungry. I hadn't eaten anything since before the attack. And I listened for the last fifteen minutes of the first leg of the flight to this couple across the aisle talking about the meatball sandwiches they get at the deli outside gate thirteen. And then the flight attendant gets on the intercom to give us flight and ground information and tells us we'll be arriving at gate thirteen. And it was like I had to have one of those sandwiches, you know? Those freaking snack packs they charge you for on the airplane wasn't going to satisfy this craving I had for what was supposedly the best meatball sandwich known to man." He sighed again. "You know the drugs they gave me in the hospital through my IV? I think maybe there were still some remnants floating around in my system because it was like their conversation had triggered a bout of the munchies. I *had* to have a meatball sandwich."

I gave him a soft giggle to keep him talking. "And so, you got off the plane to get to the meatballs."

"Yeah, and the bread, too. I knew I should have enough time to run in, grab a sandwich, and re-board. I asked the agent and the Secretary of the Interior if they wanted one, but they didn't."

I looked over to George for verification, and he nodded. "Then what happened?"

"I got the sandwich, grabbed a drink — 'cause, you know they only give you those small drinks on the plane and this was a big sandwich and those little cans weren't going to cut it — and started back for the gate. But once I had the gate in sight, I got a knot in my stomach. Like a... a big ball of dread. You know what I mean?"

"Like you couldn't get on the plane?"

"Yeah! It hit me out of nowhere. I stopped in a store 'cause... 'cause I don't know why, but I did. In the store, I didn't feel it any more. It was weird. I looked back at the gate and I was okay. So, I started towards it again. But, as I got closer, it started hitting me again. It was like everything in me was screaming at me to not get back on that plane. I couldn't make my feet take me back to the gate... I just kinda found myself getting on the escalator."

"Damn," I said, trying to keep him rambling. I looked over to Will and shook my head.

Will shrugged his shoulders.

It was Jared's voice, but he wasn't speaking like Jared.

"I know, right? But I still had the phone and I knew you were waiting for it. So, I rented a car to drive it back," he said.

"Why didn't you call somebody?"

"...My first instinct was to just get away from the airport. The whole place was starting to creep me out. I just felt... unsafe, you know?"

"But why haven't you called since?"

"Because my phone is dead and the charger was in my bag on the plane! I don't know what's going on! They're following me, I can feel it!"

"If your phone is dead, how are you talking to me now?"

"Because I found some money in my wallet and I got a charger in the place next to where I got food, before I went into the FedEx place next door. Hey! Did you get the phone? Because I sent you the phone!"

"Yeah, thanks, I got the phone. Who's following you?"

"I don't know! I thought they were going to come up and crash me to get to me. But they didn't, so I thought they were just going to wait for me to stop for the night or something and grab me then. So, I kept going."

"How's your gas tank doing?"

"It had a full tank when I took it and it's one of those hybrids. I'm getting freaking awesome gas mileage! The car's all shiny and new."

I made a noise halfway between a laugh and a sigh. "Honey, did the doctor give you any shiny, new pills for you to take with you?"

"Yes, he did! They're these little white pills that aren't as strong as the stuff they gave me in the hospital! That way I could work and help out when I got back."

"Are they a kind of pill you've taken before?"

"No... but I've never been shot before, either."

Somewhere, in the otherwise silent room, it sounded like someone just slapped their own forehead.

"And then I heard on the radio that the plane got landed on an Army base," Jared said. "Something happened on that plane... did anyone get hurt?"

"No, everyone is fine."

"But what happened?"

"A dude had diarrhea and wouldn't stay in his seat."

"Whoa."

"I know."

"I thought it was the next attempt from whoever has the President, you know? And then I really figured the ones following me were going to snag me, so I had to separate myself from the phone, 'cause maybe they were after the phone, you know?"

"Yeah, I know."

"Yo, did you get the phone?"

I smiled into the receiver. "Yeah, thanks."

"Cool."

"Where are you going now?"

"Back to the White House, duh. I'm trying to make them think I'm headed somewhere else, but I'm coming."

"Sweetie, you're stoned."

"Nuh-uh. Doc said I could work."

"I think he either got your dosage wrong, or you're having a bad reaction to the new med."

"But I feel fine."

"I'm sure you do. But you sound like an idiot."

There was a long pause as he processed that. "What do you think I should do?"

"Pull over, dude."

"I can't! I'm being followed!" he was back to sounding desperate.

"Okay, listen. When you disappeared from the airport, you made the Secret Service think that you were trying to give them the slip."

"But there weren't any agents assigned to me! I was on my own! No one was protecting me, that one guy was there for the Secretary!"

"Oh, my God, Jared!" I was starting to lose my patience with him. "You dropped off the grid in possession of the one thing that might help us figure out who took the President. The minute that plane took off without you, you became a suspect."

There was nothing but silence on the other end of the phone.

"Did you hear me? You are a suspect in the kidnapping of the President of the United States."

"But I don't have him!"

Right then and there, I decided that I was going to make it my mission to federally legalize marijuana, because right now, I felt the need to get high. A drink just wasn't going to cut it anymore. "*Our* guys are tailing you. The FBI has been following you at a distance. I need you to pull over and let them get you in their car. They'll bring you back, sober you up, and question you. Once you're cleared, you can go home and finish recuperating."

"But..." he let out a big sigh.

"Trust me, I'm not steering you wrong. If you pull over on your own, you'll be downgraded from 'suspect' to 'person of interest'. Pull. Over."

"Stay on the phone with me?"

"Absolutely. I'm right here. Pull over."

The FBI Director nodded and dialed a number on his own phone and moved to the corner of the room to start talking to his people.

He pulled over, and we waited. "I see them! They're pulling up behind me!"

"You don't have to squeal into my ear. It's okay."

"I want them to hold their badges up when they get out and come for me! I want to know they're us!"

I looked over at the Director with raised eyebrows and he gave me a nod. "Okay, no problem. They'll hold up their badges. Just don't run or drive off. If they pulled in behind you, then they are trusting you not to take off. Do not make them chase you down."

"If I hit the gas, are they going to shoot me?"

"Probably."

"Oh, *maaaaan*!"

I couldn't help it, I chuckled. "Take the key out of the ignition."

"When I see the badges. Wait... I see the badges."

"Good, now take the key out of the ignition."

"How do I know they're FBI badges?"

"No one else knows to hold up their badges on their approach. It's the FBI, trust me. Now take the key out of the ignition and follow their instructions. Come on, Jared, this is important."

"All... all right."

"Just do what they ask and I'll wait on the phone."

In the end, they got him out of his rental and into custody. The first thing they did was take his pill bottle away. The second was to sweet talk him into disconnecting the call with me. The conversation I heard going on in the backseat of that car had been hilarious.

I used two fingers to rub my forehead. When I pulled my hand away, they were oily. Man, I needed a shower.

"He could have faked all that," the FBI Director said.

"I know," I said with a tired sigh.

"It's a perfect cover. He dodges the plane, so he isn't on it when the next attack goes down. Then he fakes a reaction to a drug that was prescribed to him, after taking a bullet trying to protect the President. Then he's let back into Washington, so he can feed the enemy more information. And he gets to be everybody's hero, seemingly loyal to both sides, and gets taken in and harbored by whichever side wins. The man is a genius."

I shot him a look. "Do you think I don't know that is all a possibility? Did you notice I told him he'd be questioned and, if cleared, released to recuperate *at home*? He's not coming back while all this is going on. In the meantime, even if he passes every test and questioning process you can think to throw at him, you guys look into his shit. Look at any personal phone records, hack into his home computer, whatever else you can think of. Don't treat him like a hostile witness. You can't prove that he's done a thing to earn that. But do check him inside and out. I also want a full blood panel ran on him. I want to know what's up with the medication. I want the results ran by one of our doctors. And if he thinks the meds weren't on the up and up, I want whatever doctor treated Jared hauled in and investigated. And regardless of the outcome, I want one of our doctors taken to Colorado and have him or her go over every chart of all of our other people, I don't care who treated them. If you find nothing, then look into the nurses. I want to make sure we don't have somebody on the enemy's side working at the hospital."

My orders seemed to satisfy him, and let him know that I was taking all the possibilities seriously. He relaxed his stance a little. "Yes, Ma'am."

The forensics guy, who had been subjected to listening to the whole cell phone call, said he was ready and asked for Dad's phone.

I gave it to him, and he handed it right back because the initial password input had timed out. *Qwe#$&123*. I handed it back to him and he applied his imitation thumbprint.

No dice.

"No problem," he said. "I've got two more here, ready to go, I'll just try another."

He handed the phone back over to me to wake back up. It had gone back to sleep when the print failed. I had to put the password in again and hand it to him again.

The second print failed, and then the third.

"I'm sorry, Ma'am, that should have worked."

"Maybe a thumbprint from his other hand?" I suggested.

"It's not likely, but if he wanted to be a bit sneaky about it, it's a possibility. I'll work on trying to find one."

I nodded to him and looked back to my table of advisors. "Did we ever find out who tipped off the press yesterday morning with the footage of my telling Dad to do the tour?"

"It came from an irate eighty-eight-year-old man who never liked you or your father's politics. He's old and in a wheelchair, but he has his memory and his mind is still sharp. We checked him out. We don't think he's connected at all, just someone thinking they were doing their own version of their civic duty. You should see his social media pages."

I shook my head before looking around the room. "Anything else at the moment?"

No one spoke up. I took that to mean I could leave. "All right. I'll be in the study."

I bee-lined for the bathroom and started stripping.

"You okay?" Will called through the door.

"Yeah. I'm just going to clean up."

"I'll have Nikki go get you some clothes."

I snorted. "Good luck with that."

19 THE PHONE, A THUMBPRINT, AND A PAIR OF TRAINEES

I was now showered, dressed, and had my hair brushed. Forget the makeup and heels. They were a foreign concept to me now.

Charlotte had brought down a pants suit for me, but had swapped the blouse out for a cotton v-neck t-shirt, and my shoes wore more like sneakers. It was quite a step up on the comfort scale than what they normally had me wearing.

I walked back into the Sit Room without the suit jacket and my wet hair hanging down, making the back of my t-shirt wet at the shoulders. And I didn't care because, going into day three, I was the one that looked the least bedraggled in the room.

The forensics guy held the phone out to me.

Qwe#$&123. It would be easier if I just gave him the freaking password. I handed it back.

He tried three samples of lifted left thumbprints, each of them failing to work. "Are you sure these are his thumbprints?" he asked.

I pulled out my cell on a sigh and dialed the number for Dad's top security guy... and then I had to stop myself. He was one of the five killed. I had to clear the number and hit the button for the head of the Secret Service, Ronald. I put him on speakerphone.

"Madam President?" he answered.

"Hey, did Jerry ever mention anything about Dad having a nighttime visitor on the side that he hid from me?"

That got a few heads in the room to turn toward me.

"You mean like how I hear tales of your new Chief of Staff making visits to you?" he asked.

"Yes." I didn't have time for embarrassment right now. But I didn't look around the room at everyone else's expressions, either. *I should have warned him he was on speakerphone.*

"No, Ma'am."

"Any female visitors to the residence during the day?" I asked.

"To my knowledge there were no female visitors at any time that would be in his bedroom, Ma'am."

"How about any male visitors?"

That earned me some raised eyebrows. But, hey, I wasn't going to assume or judge anything. I just wanted to get to the bottom of it.

"No, Ma'am."

"All right. Thank you."

"Thank you, Ma'am."

I hung up and yelled for George.

"Ma'am," he said when he walked in and held up his phone, "I'm getting some very interesting texts from my boss."

I smiled, Ronald was known for working fast. "Did you ever hear of any persons visiting any of the bedrooms in the residence, except for mine?"

"No, Ma'am, no one."

"Thank you," I said, effectively dismissing him.

I turned to the forensics guy. "Unless the maid has been dipping into Dad's stash of nighttime junk food, or Lincoln's ghost has, the prints are his."

He nodded and looked over at the tech guy, "Can you pull up the maid's prints?"

"Sure thing," the tech guy replied and started tapping more keys on his keyboard. He displayed them on the wall.

The forensics dude glanced back and forth between the prints he had, and the maid's. "They don't match, which means these have to be Cartwright's. Any prints from whoever handled the bag, before the President got a hold of them, would be smudged over or incomplete at this point."

"So..." I said.

"So, the phone isn't accepting a lifted print. It should work the way I was doing it, but it's realizing the difference for some reason."

I sighed and shook my head. "Thanks for trying."

He handed the phone back to me. "I'm sorry I couldn't help you. With your permission, I'll discuss it with a few colleagues, in both forensics and tech, and see if we can't come up with something else to try."

"Permission granted. Thank you."

"Thank you," he said and left.

I stood there, holding Dad's phone, lamenting the fact that I might have a key to solving this massive puzzle in my hand, and yet I couldn't access it. This is what drove me nuts about technology. "It's taking everything in me to not crack this thing open, with a hammer, to get the card out."

"It'll wipe," the tech guy said. "It's designed to destroy information if its internal seal is broken."

"How many times can we try getting into it before it figures out it's being hacked into?"

"You can try as many times as it takes, so long as you only stumble on one access point. Now that you've stumbled over the print, if you manage finally to get past it, you can't stumble over the facial recognition. It is programmed to be very lenient in a given phase so, if greasy fingers or a tricky password gives you trouble, all is not lost. A second area of problems will tip it off, though. You'll have three chances to get the facial features passed, then you're done."

"Okay."

"And the face has to be three-dimensional. You can't just put a life-sized picture in front of it and expect it to let you in."

I smiled. "I know."

"Ma'am... How are you going to get in without him here?"

I shook my head. "Uh-uh. I'm not giving away my secret unless I get a chance to use it."

"The Halloween masks?" Will asked.

We'd all had those plastic President masks made with Dad's face for last Halloween and then spent the day torturing him with them.

"They're plastic and shiny and light won't bounce off of them right. They won't work," Will warned.

I turned and gave him a frowny face, "Oh, darn. Now I'll have to figure out a plan B."

"Ma'am," Sam said, hanging up a phone and gesturing to the wall, "our two guys are ready."

I drew my hands up and shook them in front of my face, as though I could fend off the onslaught. "Aaahhhhh!" It was one thing after another, after another, after another! Ma'am, Ma'am, Ma'am, Ma'am, *Ma'am!* The way things kept slapping me across the face, I was afraid of getting whiplash.

People stared at me while I rolled my head around, stretching my neck and shoulder muscles. I lifted my head, took a deep breath, and made a show of sitting in my chair and leaning back to get it to recline. "All right, let's roll."

An image appeared of the fake Canadian. Orange jumpsuit, elbows propped on the table he sat in front of, shackles chaining his ankles. Someone had freed his hands to eat the meal the previous team had thought might loosen his tongue. It hadn't. He looked tired, bored, and resigned.

My attention was drawn to an image that appeared on the sidewall. It was an image from the outside of the room that that held the prisoner. Our two guys had changed out of their fatigues, and were helping each other put the final additions on their all black outfits, which included facemasks.

Someone held up a hand and did a five-fingered countdown.

Then, all of a sudden, eight guys in all manner of military uniforms started shouting and throwing themselves against walls. Someone pulled out a gun and fired — what I sincerely hoped were blanks — at the ceiling. Someone else was squirting ketchup on the walls.

They definitely had my attention.

They had the non-Canadian's, as well. Shock and confusion registered on his face as he stared at the door.

Sam winked at me when I glanced at him. — I hadn't even known the man knew how to wink.

All fell silent, with the eight men now sprawled at random around the outer area.

Our two masterminds nodded to each other, popped the door to the room open, and stalked inside.

I turned back to the big screen upfront to see that our prisoner hadn't moved an inch, but his eyes sure were scanning the bodies in the hall.

The twosome came in, talking to each other in, what I assumed was, very rapid Korean. As they moved and looked for... whatever they seemed to be looking for, they pretended to not even notice the prisoner.

Buddy boy in the chair wasn't looking so bored anymore.

They turned to the prisoner. They smiled at the sight of him and continued their conversation as though the prisoner wasn't even there. Then they fell silent. One of them made a slow circle around the prisoner.

The unsub slowly drew himself up in the chair and did his best to look concerned, but not scared.

Our guy in front of the prisoner said something in the tone of a taunt.

Our guy behind the prisoner whispered something that sounded menacing and then faked a lunge.

Buddy boy jumped up and lashed out at the guy behind him, but only made contact with air. He tried to go after the guy, but his feet were still shackled to the heavy chair and it wouldn't budge.

Both of our guys laughed at him. They uttered more taunts and menacing growls at the prisoner.

...And then our prisoner began to respond. In Korean.

"What dialect is he speaking?" I asked the room, half scared of the answer.

"It's being analyzed," Sam whispered.

The clenching in my stomach told me that my gut was pretty sure it already knew.

Our twosome on the screen was now role-playing. One of them stood with his back to the corner of the room, holding a martial arts position and looking all focused and deadly. The second one was obviously asking all the questions. And he was doing it in a manner that clearly implied his curiosity was the only thing keeping the prisoner alive.

"Exactly what game are they playing?" I asked.

"Hold on," Sam said with a raised finger.

Our friend in the chair may not have feared a quick death by gun that other military officers threatened. But he certainly didn't embrace the idea of a long martial arts death from these two. The sullen man in the corner looked like he was the type that liked to play around with his prey before going in for the kill.

"Sir," the tech guy said.

Sam turned his head.

The tech guy nodded.

"Shit," Sam muttered under his breath.

My stomach clenched even tighter.

"Both of our two guy's families come from South Korea," Sam said. "They're very aware that South Korea wants to maintain their good relationship with the US."

"Because of the tenuous position that North Korea, with their nukes and inability to comply with UN regulations, puts them in," I said.

"Right. When they saw that he looked markedly Korean, they took a gamble that he was from one side of the border, or the other."

"So, they're pretending to be from Korea themselves."

"Yes, South Korea. They pretended to kill the Americans guarding the room because it was a necessary step in showing that not only are they more powerful and skilled than a dozen soldiers, but that they can take their time with him and not bat an eyelash. They figured that if they put on a big enough show, they could shock him into cracking. If the guy turned out to be North Korean, he'd want to give the two Southies a set-down, taunt them a little with the plan, and tell them that killing him won't stop the ultimate plan. If the guy turned out to be from South Korea, they'll tell him that they're there to annihilate the threat to the alliance between South Korea and the US. Either way, they figured they could start out by bluffing a bit."

I scrunched my eyebrows together. "What was their excuse for killing the soldiers, if they represent our allies?"

"They wanted to destroy any proof of their involvement or interference. South Korea wanted to be able to get the information out of this guy and offer it to the US, so they could be seen as valuable."

"But —"

"The man's going to buy into it because things are happening so fast. He doesn't have time to stop and think it through too much..." His expression shifted as he realized what he'd done, "Sorry to interrupt you, Ma'am."

I waved it off. "And so? Is he from the North, or South?"

"He's from North Korea."

I gripped the armrests on the chair as the Earth shifted its axis. It suddenly felt like we were now spinning in some other, unnatural, way. "Is the guy he's working for North Korean?"

The tech guy was looking at a live feed of a translated transcript of the conversation going on. "Yes, Ma'am."

"Oh, my God." I was in serious danger of throwing up.

"Is he working on behalf of the North Korean government?" Sam asked the tech guy.

"He says he doesn't know who the boss works for, he only has the one man as a point of contact. He doesn't even know if the guy he's been talking to is the one that has the President, or if the guy just wanted to strike while we already had so much going on." The tech guy paused for a moment to scan more of the transcript. "He was given a flight number and pictures of the two US government workers and was told to kill either one. He was going to kill one with his bare hands and then understood that he'd be shot dead by the Secret Service agent."

"Why was he willing to commit himself to a suicide mission, if he didn't even know who the ultimate boss was?" I asked.

"Because he was promised that his family would be paid millions on his behalf, if the American government was brought down."

"And killing a person on the plane was to achieve what?" I asked.

"To create panic within the public. If they could panic a country as large as ours, it would make an impression on the rest of the world."

I turned back to Sam. "What have the North Korean military movements been like since the incident?"

"Unusually quiet."

I turned to the Secretary of State with a questioning look on my face.

"North Korea made contact with us, simply denying responsibility," he said. "Whether it was truthful or not, I don't know. What I do know is they expressed no sympathy."

"Ma'am," Sam said, "all this could really be coming from them. They could be using this little, unknown guy to hide behind. Their thought being that we'd be looking for this little guy, and by the time we found their decoy, they'd swoop in with something just as we were patting ourselves on the back."

"And if he isn't working with the government?"

"If that man is in North Korea, and North Korea finds out, they'll race us to find him, and they'll keep him. If for no other reason than to lord it over our heads and question him on how he managed to pull off so much."

I was starting to feel dizzy. "They'll pull us into a war."

"And a war with them all but guarantees that it'll be nuclear."

"We *have* to figure out where the kidnapper is holed up at, especially if he may not be hooked up with the government yet."

"The next time he makes contact, we'll narrow the search down to North Korea, specifically. If he's there, it'll speed up our ability to unscramble the location of the signal. With any luck, we might be able to rule it out as a possibility."

My mouth went dry. I didn't want to live through a nuclear war, let alone be in charge of leading one. I stood up, my intent to go into the office and vomit or pass out or something equally as embarrassing and weak, but I had to stop and grip onto the back of the chair for support, instead.

Everyone was looking at me, waiting for me to say something, to give them a direction in which to head. They were waiting for me to lead them. Either that or I looked as bad as I felt and they were waiting for me to break down and quit.

"I need a secure conference call set up. I have to talk to the Speaker of the House and the President Pro Tempore. I need to prepare them for what we may be facing," I said as my nails continued to dig in.

"Ma'am, you know what you'll have to do if we end up in a war with North Korea," Sam warned.

I took a deep breath. "Yes."

"Are you going to wait for them to strike first?"

I flexed my fingers into the chair's back cushion. "We'll have to see how this plays out."

"If they strike first, you know damned right well where they'll strike."

"Yes, I do. If they launch, we'll have a minute amount of time for me to launch before we're obliterated. I don't need Congress to declare war in order to defend the country. Besides, it's not as though any of us will be around for anyone to try to impeach me. But if you're looking for me to order an attack first, Congress will have to declare it."

"Do you want to adjust the aim of some of the missiles?"

Ugh, I couldn't believe I was really talking about doing this... "I think they'll see that as a direct threat. It's a premature move. However, that said, I want the system drilled on a plan to determine where each missile should be re-aimed to strike, and how many missiles it will take to wipe them off the face of the Earth. I want to know how long it takes to reposition the missiles and get them launched. I want to know how much time we'll have between finding out they're coming and when impact will be. In other words, make very quiet preparations. Because I tell you all this, if they launch against us, it'll be the last thing that country ever does."

"Do you plan on being that aggressive if Congress ends up declaring war and we take the offense?"

"No. I'll be out to wipe the government, military bases, and any nuclear launch locations. The public won't like it. They'll hate it. But if we don't, the

North Koreans will do it to us."

"You'll incite the wrath of their allies."

I sighed at him. It seemed as though Sam was single-handedly trying to play both good-cop and bad-cop. "Maybe, maybe not," I said. "They aren't the only ones with allies. Nuclear war is going to mean the end of life, for many of us. And we won't go down without a fight. With any luck, their allies will back down if North Korea no longer exists to help them."

"You will humor us and let us kick around a few ideas and present them to you, right?"

I blew out a breath in an effort to make the room stop spinning. "Of course. Run some scenarios. Get some intelligence together. And get some updated satellite images. Figure out who our greatest threats, and biggest allies, would be if we end up having to do this."

"Yes, Ma'am. When will you contact the UN?"

"As soon as we know for sure it's North Korea."

"Yes, Ma'am."

"If you'll excuse me..." I left and went into the office.

Will walked in just as I finished hurling into the trashcan. He sighed behind me and pulled out his phone. "I'm going to get the doctor over here to check you out."

I grabbed a few tissues. "No, I'm just stressed and dehydrated. And starving myself, apparently, because nothing but bile came up." I'd quit picking at the bite-sized buffet at some point in this mess.

"Sorry, babe. If the President vomits, the President must be seen by the doctor."

"Ugh." I took a small amount of satisfaction in the idea that at least he hadn't called me Ma'am.

And then I watched him tap and swipe, and tap his password, and press his thumbprint, and do the selfie... and I flopped to the floor from the force of my epiphany.

20 THE DOCTOR AND THAT CLEVER THUMBPRINT

Will ran out of the room, through the Sit Room, and flung the hallway door open, "PRESIDENT DOWN!"

Men flew at me. One second I was sitting on the floor by myself, and the next I was surrounded, again, by a wall of male muscle. Their quick movements made my head swim. I grabbed the trashcan and threw up again.

George started patting me down, "Are you hit?"

"No," I said, wiping my mouth with my fistful of tissues.

"Did you eat or drink anything that wasn't from inside the Sit Room?"

I had to think about that. "A bottle of water."

"Where'd you get it from?" He stood me up and studied my face.

"The mini-fridge in the Oval's study."

"Was anything out of place in that room?"

"No... I don't know. I just went in there to look in the notebook again for a page that might have Dad's cell phone password written on it. I just reached over, opened the door, and grabbed it. I didn't even really look inside the fridge."

He got me whisked up in his arms and started shouting out orders like I was about to die on his watch.

Someone else opened up the door to the study and George put me down on the couch and knelt beside me. He started talking about getting a bunker analysis done and asking them to check and make sure there was enough oxygen getting down here. Someone asked if George wanted to evacuate me. Someone else shouted for the doctor. And yet another person handed George a black, zippered pack.

George unzipped the small bag and whipped out a needle, freaking preparing to stick me with it.

"Whoa!" I yelled through a scratchy throat. "Hands off, now!"

George's hands dropped and everyone froze.

"What's in the syringe?" I asked, snapping out of my sensory stupor.

"Nothing. I'm going to do a blood draw. We need to know what's in your system."

"Nothing's in my system, that's the problem. I haven't eaten, and it's taken me all day just to get down half a bottle of water. My blood sugar probably dropped."

"Somebody go out there and get her a fruit plate," George commanded. Then he held up the syringe. "You're probably right, but you're still going to let me draw some blood so we can do a quick screening on it."

I dry-heaved. Nothing came up, but it sure made George jump back. "Fine."

He did the draw and jotted down screenings on a clipboard. Blood gases, toxicology screening, blood sugars, and a few other things that I couldn't read from my angle were all included.

The doctor arrived in time to look over the paper and add a pregnancy test to the list.

I sighed.

The doctor cleared all the extra people out of the room but let Will and George stay.

Someone handed George the fruit plate before leaving the room. George didn't know if the doctor would want me to have it before he was done asking his questions or not, so he ended up just holding it.

The doctor was no stranger to me. He was the one that had been in charge of my care for the last year and a half. "All right, what happened?" Caleb asked.

"I was getting stressful news and my stomach started cramping. The conversation kept going on and I ended up getting dizzy and lightheaded. I went into the office, out there, and threw up a couple times. I haven't eaten much since Dad disappeared and nothing today. I haven't been drinking much, either. And I have more fingers on one hand than I've had hours of sleep the past two nights."

Caleb reached over, took the plate out of George's hand, and gave it to me. "The absolute worst thing you can do right now is to not take care of your body. You can't protect any of us if I have to admit you to a hospital."

I sighed and started eating, even though food seemed to be the last thing my stomach wanted.

Caleb started pulling things out of his bag and set up an IV.

"What about when you dropped to the floor?" Will asked.

"Oh!" I tried to stand up in my enthusiasm but six hands rushed to push me back down.

"Stay down," Caleb said as he extended my arm out and started looking for a good vein to assault.

"Why are you about to poke me?"

"I'm going to get you rehydrated and drip a vitamin pouch into you. It's quicker than fighting with you to eat and drink. Moreover, you're less likely to throw this back up if we skip the stomach. Now, what made you drop?"

"The phone!" I looked towards Will. "I watched you hold your phone in your right hand and use your thumb to go through all the safety features."

"Yeah, so?" Will asked.

"Memories of Dad doing his flashed through my mind. He always held it with two hands when going through the security features. I never really thought about it before, he's been playing trombone with papers and electronics for years when he doesn't have his reading glasses on. He holds the thing he's reading with two hands as he's trying to gauge the correct distance to hold it. And then it dawned on me that he didn't always tap with his right thumb."

"But the left thumb didn't match," Will said.

"I know. He'd hold the phone in both hands. His forefingers on each side, the back of it resting on his middle fingers, with the other fingers hanging down, and used his left thumb to balance the front while he maneuvered the screen with the right thumb. I can picture him using his right thumb to tap it awake, swipe, and tap in the password."

"And then what?"

"And then he'd tap the screen with his *left forefinger*, and then he'd hold the phone up for the facial recognition. I just always thought the left forefinger thing was just the way he changed hand positions to lift the phone up for the facial part. But he must have been using that print instead of the thumb."

"But, why?"

"Because that's just how he is. His password is stupid, there's nothing clever about it. And I know his facial recognition is on the fuzziest setting because his beard and mustache would give it fits. But, he wasn't stupid, nor did he take security lightly. It only makes sense that he'd pick one part to be clever about. Who the heck would guess he'd use the forefinger of his non-dominant hand?"

"Oh. My. God. I always knew he was smart, but damn," Will breathed.

"His facial recognition is set to fuzzy... because he was fuzzy?" Caleb asked with a smirk.

That got a half-chuckle from me. "Kind of. You can adjust the setting of how much detail the program looks for. The more detail, the less tolerant of expression and hair changes it is. His beard would get steadily scruffier and bushier as the day wore on. Rather than have to try more than once to get it to recognize him, he just set it on the least detailed setting. I know because we had this big, frustrated conversation about the program when they put it on our phones. It was driving us nuts, trying to get it just right a hundred times a day. So, they showed us how to change the setting."

"Is that why you're so sure you can get past that part?" Will asked.

"Yep."

"Are you planning to use his portrait hanging upstairs? It's large enough to capture detail. ...It's still only two-dimensional, it won't work."

"I'm telling you, I can get past it. Just call forensics and get them back over here."

"What's on the phone?" Caleb asked.

"We want to look at his text messages. We're trying to find out if anyone planted the idea to stop at that overlook into his head. The only people who should have known were the ones in the car with him. But someone on the outside knew he'd be there."

"What about texts the others in the car were sending?" Caleb asked.

"At this point, we've checked the phones of the others who were in the car with him. Their texts are clean, or at least they were by the time we got to them. The Secretary has passed his lie-detector test and questioning. They're working on Jared now." I started picking at the fruit.

"As long as your blood work comes back all right, you can get back at it as soon as those pouches are emptied."

"Can you add another pouch?" I asked.

"Of what?"

"Caffeine."

"Uh, no. I'm not setting up a caffeine drip. It'll dehydrate you even more and end up making your heart race. George will end up calling me back in here to check you out for a heart attack."

I responded by sticking my tongue out at him.

He walked over to the fridge and got me a fresh bottle of water. "I know you're not going to sleep right for a long while coming, but you're going to have to eat and drink. And I know you're under an incredible amount of stress and worry, but if I have to admit you into the hospital, someone else is going to have to run the show."

"I know."

"Now, I don't think anyone has ever had to ask the President this question before, but —"

"Fifteen days ago. I knew you were going to ask, I already did the math in my head."

"Well, good. One less thing to worry about."

"You ain't kidding." The last thing I needed at my age, and with my new job title, was a baby. I could see the headlines now.

George had left once the blood tests had come back in agreement with my own diagnosis. Will was in the outer office, speaking on the phone,

Caleb was beginning to pack up because the IV bags were about empty, and I was watching TV and reading text messages.

I was learning more and more about Jared's progress. And they kept e-mailing portions of translated transcripts of the fake-Canadian's ongoing questioning, so I was up-to-date with that, as well.

Unfortunately, what I was watching on TV was closed-circuit coverage of our press secretary getting her ass handed to her.

She was maintaining control, but it was tenuous at best. The people weren't being given answers and it was pissing them off. I couldn't find it in myself to blame them.

If I had the luxury of being a regular citizen right now, I'd be pissed as hell that we didn't know who our enemy was yet. We were nearing the seventy-two-hour mark and the only lead we had was aiming at a very ugly place. I swear I hoped everything we thought we knew was wrong.

They were now on to questioning Chelsea as to why the doctor had been seen coming into the building by three separate witnesses.

I had half a notion to grab my IV bags and carry them upstairs and into the press briefing room. I wondered what the hell their reaction to that would be. It probably wouldn't be pretty.

Those people were out for blood. They wanted the captor's, but it was beginning to look as though they'd settle for anything that was red.

It made me want to send them vats of ketchup.

The pouches finished dripping and Caleb left.

I went back into the Sit Room, in search of more food. It seemed that taking some time to relax had unclenched my stomach enough to feel hungry.

People looked at me when I started gathering a couple of the small meatballs and a deviled egg on a small plate, but I ignored them.

As if on cue, the chef entered and caught me at the buffet. His face lit up. "Perhaps there's something in particular I could make for you?" he asked.

"This is fine, thank you."

"No, really. Anything. The kitchen staff is going nuts. We want to help in any way we can."

I gave him a cocky grin. "Could you poison the press for me? We can just blame it on the guys who took Dad."

He smiled. "Please don't tempt me."

"Well... my Mom used to make these amazing hot dogs for parties. She'd cut them into fourths and wrap half a strip of bacon around each piece and pinned it together with a toothpick. Then she'd sprinkle brown sugar on them and bake them."

His smile broadened. "I know just what you're talking about, Ma'am. I'm on it."

"And sweet tea," I called after him.

"Yes, Ma'am," he said over his shoulder, and disappeared around the corner of the doorway.

"Those hot dog things sound pretty good," Sam said.

"It's amazing how grease and sugar still sound tolerable even when you can't stand the thought of food," I said.

"It's not weak to be human, Ma'am."

I snorted. "Sure, it is."

"You're not a soldier. It is okay to need a few moments every now and again."

I looked him in the eye. "No, I'm not a soldier. I just command them. Could you please not try to make me feel justified in hitting the deck?"

"Yes, Ma'am."

"Ma'am?" the forensics guy, who was now back in his claimed corner of the room, said. "I'm sorry, I am. But I can't get a complete print off this bag."

I took a deep breath, trying not to snap at the guy who was trying to do his job. "We can get someone to take you back upstairs so you can look for another source of prints."

"Yes, Ma'am," he said.

"Check the bathroom drawers."

"Yes, Ma'am."

"Go out and tell George what you need."

"Yes, Ma'am."

I sat down and picked at my plate for a moment before I threw half a meatball back down on the dish. "What is this asshole waiting for?!"

"Well, if he's trying to wear you down, he's winning," Sam said with a pointed look.

"Yeah, but he wouldn't know that."

"He could be waiting for the higher ups to signal him, if he's working for somebody else. Or, he's still waiting to hear from a minion about another snagging or kill."

My head turned to a side screen, where I could see that Chelsea was still trying to keep her head above water. "When was our last head count?"

"No one else has gone missing. The air force is about a half hour out in getting our first wave of survivors back to DC. At that point, you'll have all your cabinet members back. The next wave will start out just as soon as the last two patients get released."

I was still staring at the screen, waiting... "We have to keep someone in the line of succession separate, away from DC."

"We'll move the Secretary of the Interior out now, before the other two get to town," Sam offered. "Where would you like him to go?"

"Midway?" I said with a sarcastic smile. "No one would think to look there. But I guess I could settle for shipping him to Camp David."

"I could have him taken to Area 51."

That got a genuine laugh from me. "Yeah, maybe the aliens can hide him on one of their planets for me." My head whipped around to Sam. "Wait... Are there aliens at Area 51?"

A familiar gleam came to his eye. "You're the President, would you like the full debriefing?"

Uhhh... "Maybe not quite yet. Let me finish dealing with this mess first. Then, yeah, I sooo want to know." I pursed my lips, trying to come up with some other ideas of where to tuck the Secretary safely away. "We could get him on a rocket and send him to the space station."

He shook his head. "Area 51 has a system of underground tunnels. It's far enough away that if DC is blown off the map, he'll be safe. And, it has a communications system like this one already in place. He'll have instant access to everything he'll need to take over at a moment's notice."

This much I had already known about. It was on the list of places the President could be moved to, if DC either had been compromised, or was too far away when something major happened. It just seemed like the obvious choice. Then again, where else would he have the full technological ability to take over? "Alright, let's get him moved."

"Yes, Ma'am." He picked up a phone to start making arrangements.

"Wait."

He paused and looked at me again.

"Let's move out the Secretary of Health and Human Services, as well. We'll tuck her away somewhere else. Everyone knows about Area 51. Let's have a Plan C in place."

Sam nodded. "Sure. We'll send Health and Human Services to...?"

"Stick her on Air Force One and keep her mobile. She can run the country from the plane, if she has to."

"Yes, Ma'am." He finished dialing and put the phone to his ear.

"Ma'am," someone called out from behind me.

I turned to see that the forensics guy was back, carrying a couple items. "You don't look very encouraged."

"Your father was right-handed, which means he picked up and moved things mainly with his right hand. That and the fact that housekeeping does a really good job with dusting and wiping everything down, means that the likelihood of finding a complete, intact print is low."

"We just need one," I said.

"It's a matter of me finding it."

"Do you want to get a team in there to dust the room?"

"Uh, Ma'am?" the Secretary of State cut in. "We haven't swept the room for classified intelligence. We don't know what Cartwright may have stuffed where."

"But," the forensics guy countered, "if you do that, you could destroy a good print. Though if it makes you feel better, Charlotte looked inside each drawer to make sure there weren't papers, or anything work related, inside before I was allowed to touch anything."

"You've already been in there twice without a full sweep," the Secretary of State said. "That's two more times than I'm comfortable with."

"Yo!" I interrupted them. "Housekeeping staff go in there all the time. What's the difference?"

"The staff members that are allowed into the private quarters have been here for years, decades. Some of them got the job because their parent held it before them, and other White House staff members have known them since they were kids and came to visit where their Daddy worked. They've already proven their loyalty. And they aren't in there to dig through drawers and papers," the Secretary of State said.

I held my hands up to hush them both. "Okay, okay, okay," I said to calm myself as much as anybody else. "Somewhere in our massive federal operation here, we must have someone with top-secret clearance, who also has the ability to sweep for fingerprints."

We all looked at each other for a moment and then all turned to the Sam's aide.

He looked shocked for a second, "Oh! You want me to search the database!" and started tapping keys.

I glanced back at the press gaggle on the screen, picked up the half meatball I'd thrown down, put it in my mouth, and went back to watching the aide.

"All right," the aide said a moment later. "We've got a few, actually."

"Good," I said. "Send one of them up there."

"Well, we don't actually have them here in the building," he said.

"So, call one and get them in here."

"Well, it'll take some time," the aide hedged.

I turned to Will, who'd finished his phone calls and had come back into the room. "That's it. I no longer have the patience for this job."

"It's just that we sent a lot of people to the Colorado site," the aide said. And the others in or around town would have to go through a lie-detector test and questioning, once they got here, before they'd be cleared to go upstairs."

I started muttering to myself. "I'm going to lose it. I've got to go hit a punching bag, or scream into the wind, or...." I spotted the press core on the screen again as one of the idiots was accusing Chelsea of covering up the whereabouts of the President. I saw red. Flames leapt at the edges of my vision. I stood and spun on the heel of my shoe and headed for the door. "Work on getting someone here," I called over my shoulder.

Out the door, up the stairs, and through hallways I went. I was in the mood for blood, and I'd found the perfect target for my hostilities.

I was gathering quite the entourage as I went, too. People had jumped up to follow in my wake. The more it became apparent where I was headed, the more they all began to protest.

I finally spun back around on them.

Everyone stopped short and some bumped into each other.

"I haven't addressed the nation in two days. They're getting anxious and rambunctious. Anybody want to tell me I really shouldn't say something, anything to them?"

"Ma'am, you should wait until a statement has been prepared," Will said.

I crossed my arms in front of myself. "Well, they've had two days, does anyone have one?"

"It was decided that Chelsea would handle them."

"Yeah, well, it looks like Chelsea could use a little help. Anybody else want to go out there and deal with it?"

No one volunteered.

Chelsea had been in front of the corps off and on for about two hours. Nothing was really making it onto the airwaves. We'd been watching everything on our closed-circuit television. Chelsea was trying to humor them by notating their questions, saying she'd run them by the team again, but no one believed she'd come back with any answers.

I stepped out into the room, people saw me, and they erupted with yelled questions. As though I was going to be able to discern any of the questions with them all screaming like spoiled toddlers denied the dessert that the adults were eating in front of them.

Chelsea couldn't decide if she was pissed at me or glad for the reprieve.

"Here, now," she said into the microphone, "the President."

As Chelsea exited to the wings, the Secretary of State entered to be that silent presence I had asked him to be at the start of all this.

As they continued to shout over each other, I looked out at the gathering of reporters and thought about how I used to have a principal in elementary school that had the most amazing talent I've ever seen.

She could walk up to the front of the auditorium, cock her hip, cross her arms, throw on a distasteful expression, and just glance around the large room. The entire population of the school would shut up. Students, staff, everyone. It was like she'd flipped a switch.

I walked up to the microphone and imitated that principal.

Suddenly, people remembered the protocol of manners around here.

When the President of the United States walks into the room, you shut the hell up and stand.

"Good evening," I began as I adjusted my stance to a more normal posture. "The last contact made by the captor was approximately thirty hours ago. At that time, I had confirmation that President James Cartwright was alive —"

"Was he harmed?" someone called out.

I cocked a hip, and an eyebrow, and eyed the one who'd talked.

I knew I was going to take flack for coming in and having this kind of attitude with the press. I know that as a citizen, my attitude in handling the press would irritate me and make me think the President was hiding something. However, this little display of mine was more about regaining the reigns of the press corps, before handing them back off to Chelsea. They all had to be made to remember that they didn't run things inside this building. I did.

"At this point," I began, and straightened to continue, "we are still reliant on the captor, or captors, to establish communication. Their technology is sophisticated and we have not cracked it, as of yet. The captor has made a ransom demand. One that requires the rearranging of our military positions, and we will not be giving into that demand, for to do so would put the country in danger. It would also endanger our position within the world scene. We do not negotiate with terrorists, period. Moreover, the captor knows that if he kills President James Cartwright, he no longer has any means of further control. Though it is important for everyone to understand that all he has right now is our attention.

"Jared, the president's personal aide is not missing, contrary to popular opinion. He is with FBI and CIA agents as we speak. He is cooperating and answering questions, and sobering up. There was a problem with his medication, which had been prescribed and filled at the hospital in Colorado. I'm told that it interacted with a separate, ongoing prescription that Jared failed to tell the doctor about at the hospital. We'll chalk that miscommunication up to the painful and nerve-wracking experience of having a gunshot wound. Once debriefed, Jared will be given time off to finish recovering from his ordeal, at home, in peace.

"I'd now like to clear up the matter of the plane incident. It is true that there was only one Secret Service agent onboard the plane, but you should also note that there were two air marshals assigned to the flight as well. The taking down of the suspect was accomplished by a joint effort. Thanks to the quick thinking of the staff onboard the flight, no persons were harmed in the incident.

"The suspect remains in custody, and questioning continues at this hour. We do believe this incident is connected to the kidnapping of the President. It was designed to be an attempt at a second life, and was successfully thwarted.

"The rumors about President James Cartwright's phone are partially true. We are in possession of the phone. Its contents are still within it. I'm working on a way to get past the security features. The question is in whom he may have been texting when he decided to make the scenic stop.

Somebody out there knew where he'd be stopping. We think the phone may be the key as to how the information got out. And while most of your phones may have records with the company as to which numbers were talking and texting when, the president's phone has no such record. The President's phone is completely untraceable, and if we try to crack into it and remove the card to put it in a reader it will self-destruct, which means that it will erase the contents. Therefore, as I've said, I'm working on getting past the security features.

"And finally, the doctor. I fell. I haven't slept, I was dehydrated, and I fell. It wasn't a big deal, I didn't hurt myself, but the President trips and they call in back up. I was given an IV with a saline solution and a vitamin pouch. And I do feel better. I was advised to sleep, but I think we all know that won't be happening anytime soon.

"As for the internal leak, we're working on it. It takes time. That fact irritates me far more than it irritates any of you, believe me. I and everybody else in the Situation Room have already been screened and questioned. We have all passed with ease and excellence. But, make no mistake, we will find the betrayer, and they will be dealt with.

"We are currently working on getting all of our people back from Colorado. We are still waiting on the release of, I believe, two patients. Then we will clear all remaining survivors from that location. Military and Secret Service personnel will remain at the incident's location to continue combing the scene. Officials have been able to put together the approach and techniques used by the abduction team. This scene is to be studied ad nauseam so that we may learn from this, and never allow it to be repeated.

"I know that I don't have all the answers you want. I have so many unanswered questions that I could put your lists to shame. The only thing I can offer you is the assurance that everything that can be done, is being done. We definitely have a suspicion, though we are not allowing that suspicion to drive our investigation. No one, and I can truly say no one, has a larger desire than I have to get to the bottom of this mess. I will find out who is responsible for this, and I will see that they are punished.

"Forgive me the rest of your questions. These are the answers that we have at this time. I can offer you no more, and for that, I am disappointed. I want answers, too. I want justice. I want heads to roll.

"For the record, we're not in possession of a time machine, I checked," then I winked. "That was a joke. I can't turn back time and make this not happen. I can't speed up time and get this finished now. All we can do is wait and work the process. I'm going to get you, and myself, answers. It's just going to take time. We all have to deal with that reality.

"On a side note, I'm open to all your prayers, well wishes, good vibes, mojo... Any positive thing you want to think in my direction, I'll take it."

That got me a chuckle.

"Anyone who can positively identify the guy who took my father, and can bring the guy to me, I'll make you a deal. I'll pardon you from having to pay income tax, ever again."

They laughed.

"That really was a joke. I can only pardon someone for a crime until my term is up. Thank you."

I left the room. I'd left them smiling and in a more relaxed atmosphere. They'd rip me apart all over the news for cracking jokes at a time like this. I was sure. But they'd been ripping us apart since about twenty-four hours after this went down. At least now, Chelsea should be able to have a better grip on control over the group.

She was waiting for me when I rounded the corner behind the wall I'd just been standing in front of.

"I don't know whether to thank you or smack you!"

I cocked an eyebrow and smiled. "I dare you to smack me."

"Ma'am —"

"You were dying out there. I watched them crucify you, repeatedly. You weren't rising to the occasion. Are you in over your head?"

Her eyes widened for a moment, and then she slumped her shoulders. "I'm in it up to my hairline.

"Well get whatever help in here you need. You have to keep the situation in that room diffused."

"I'm just not used to going for so long with nothing to give them."

"I understand. I just gave them everything I have."

"Thank you. I should be able to handle it now. I'll be able to kill the rest of the day backtracking your tax statement and the crack about the time machine."

"Well then, my job here is done."

"Yes, Ma'am."

21 THE FEDEX PACKAGE

I ran into Sam's aide in the hallway.

"Ma'am, we have contact!"

"Hahaha! I knew that press conference would get to him. Let's go," I said, picking up the pace.

We ran down the hall. The whole time, I knew Will wanted to say something to me about my impromptu press conference. Yet, he knew we had more important things to deal with right now.

It was as we rode down on the elevator that I finally acknowledged the part of me that just wanted to lay my eyes on Dad one more time. I kept trying to tell myself that I might be rushing to the Sit Room just to be presented with the image of his body. But I still wanted to see him. My deepest, darkest fear was that they had killed him and would just cease contacting us at all, knowing they didn't have anything to bargain with, and they would decide to leave us forever wondering about what had happened.

I did a calmer fast-walk from the elevator to the Sit Room and tried to enter with some sense of decorum.

I went straight over to the desk, looking up at the video feed that was showing me nothing but peeling ceiling tiles.

"You ready?" Sam asked.

"No." I kicked off my shoes, leaned back in the chair, propped my feet up on the desk, and then gave a nod. "Ready."

There was about a four second delay between the time I saw our live feed go up on the side wall and when the camera was moved and refocused on the same old, same old. Idiot man on the left, beat up Dad on the right.

I gave him my best impression of boredom, while on the inside I was sighing with relief.

"It's been an exciting day for you, Princess."

"So now you're changing my title?"

"Daddy gets taken from the throne and female child takes over, is that not a Princess?"

"Not in this country." Actually, that would be a queen, you twit.

"Then what would you call yourself?"

"Massively connected. But everyone else insists on calling me the President."

Dad managed a small smile. Funny how my never-ending sense of sarcasm hadn't amused him when I was a teenager. But, then again, we both knew that no matter what was happening, if we could find amusement in it somewhere, anywhere, we could somehow find the strength to keep on going. It had been a lesson we had both learned well.

My sarcasm and his smile let each of us know the other was holding it together... Even if it was mostly out of a desire to not fail the other.

"Be that as it may, Princess," the captor said, drawing my attention back to him, "I'm sorry to hear you haven't been eating or sleeping." And then he smirked.

I smirked back. "Yeah, it's been real exhausting making all my plans now that I've secured the presidency. The two years left in Dad's term aren't going to be enough for me to accomplish all I want to do, now that you've put me in charge. I'm already making election plans. I've gotta keep my throne." Then I paused and offered him a wink. — Hey, if he had superiors, and they were watching, it wouldn't hurt me none to make them suspicious that their man might be two-faced.

"Little child, I've done you no favors, save one."

"Yeah, and it's a big one. You got me into this chair."

"No. You'll not run that country your way. I will bend you to my will. You will deliver to me my demands."

I wrinkled my brow. "Who taught you English?"

He looked slightly insulted. "My English is more proper than yours."

I snorted. "Not in this country."

"The culture of your country is pathetic. You value all the wrong things."

"And yet, you're the one wanting a favor from us. And why? Because you don't have the power to accomplish your goals on your own."

He started laughing. "The power I have would amaze you."

"Then why do you need our cooperation so damn bad?"

"We want you out of the way!"

Now we might be getting somewhere. "So, you can do what with all your power?"

"You nosey Americans, always having to know what everyone else is doing. Move your ships so I can be done with you!"

I could only shake my head and chuckle at the situation. I was now gathering that 'we' didn't actually want to pick a fight with the US directly. It now looked like they planned on going after a smaller fish in the sea. The question was what country were they actually after? "Who's 'we'?" I asked.

"Never you mind. Move your vessels. I don't have to give you your father back, if you don't want him. You can have your coup. Now, in return, you do me the favor of helping me. We can be allies."

I smiled at him as though we had just reached a new level of understanding with one another. "If I move the fleet, I can't *not* get him back. I'd have to take him back, and then I'd lose the throne I'm sitting on. And now that my father has sat there and heard all this, he'd end me if he comes back. Don't you see? I'm stuck. I cannot help you. But I thank you kindly for your help in obtaining my new title."

He narrowed his eyes on me, switching to a new tact. "Did you receive my package?"

My brow lifted in surprise. "You sent me a package? How sweet of you."

"The Federal Express site says it has been delivered to the White House fifteen minutes ago. Have you not been presented with it, yet? I wanted to watch you open it."

I fought the urge to let my eyes dart over to the others in the room. "Any packages have to be screened. It could be a while before it's placed in my hands."

"Pity."

"You could just tell me what's in it."

"And ruin the surprise? I think not. Let us just say that I've sent you a little something to remember your Daddy by."

"A lock of hair, maybe?"

He smiled. "Sweet dreams, Princess," he said, and then disconnected.

Our connection was cut soon after. The group surrounding the edges of the room remained quiet for a moment. I could only imagine that their thoughts were running much like my own...

"Is he in North Korea?" I asked my favorite tech guy.

"Yes, Ma'am."

"Did you get a location while I bantered?"

"Yes, a general one."

"Why are you not smiling?"

He flashed his teeth at me in a fleeting grin. "We have it narrowed down to a fifteen-mile radius."

"Get satellites all over the area. We have to heat-seek... Can we get drones in there?"

Will grinned at my impatience to get something going. Sam grimaced.

The tech guy put maps of the radius up on the screens, so we could see exactly what we were dealing with.

"There's a military installation within that radius. And while that gives us a good place to start looking, you don't want to fly drones in there," Sam said.

My emotions had just ridden a hellacious roller coaster in the course of the last couple of exchanges. Getting the location narrowed down started to paint pictures of a rescue effort in my head. But the news of the military installation just turned those images into nightmare fodder. There wouldn't be a rescue mission. I admonished myself for even entertaining the momentary hope. Hope would lead to disappointment, and I was disappointed enough already. Disappointment would eventually lead to heartache, and I couldn't afford that emotion right now.

"Was he truthful about just wanting us out of the way or was he bluffing, thinking that it might get us to cooperate?" I asked.

"Does it matter?"

"It might."

"You thinking of giving in, Ma'am?" he asked with a pointed look.

I resisted the urge to roll my eyes and held my gaze steady. "I'm thinking a lot of things. I'm thinking that I need to know what all of my options are. I'm thinking there's a little something to the idea of letting another country take care of itself. Although, there's something to be said for protecting a country that is incapable of doing it for themselves, especially if it plays by the UN's rules and the enemy country doesn't. I'm thinking that if they are after a potential enemy of ours, to maybe not interfere and let them have at it. But, if it's an ally, we need to hold our position or our other allies will doubt our loyalties. I'm also thinking that it could all be a lie and they'll say anything to get us to move out so they can position themselves for the real show. Either way, if we aren't the target, it's only good manners to alert the country that is in the crosshairs."

"Analysis of the body language and facial expressions says he was lying," Sam's assistant said as he read incoming reports on his computer screen.

"Even if they are after a smaller country, his lying would still make sense. They'd be looking for any opportunity to put a dent in us," I said.

"Meaning if you backed out to let them have at the other country, they'd still make a move against us and the rest of the world would see how we bowed down to them," Sam said.

"Would you relax?" I asked. "I'm taking notes for the UN. You think I'm not going to report anything and everything I can? We've been watching North Korea for years. I want the world to know of their intended actions, just as soon as we fully figure out what they are."

"Now," I said, turning to Will, "where's the package? What's in it?"

"It's probably in a pile with whatever else we received with the shipment. I'll call up and see if they can locate it."

"Too bad he probably put a fake return address on it," the Sam quipped.

"FedEx is going to politely start declining any packages being addressed for this place, if news stories about this begin to get associated with them," I added.

"Oh, nah," the Sam drawled out. "Once this guy's recordings hit cyber space, everything will get pinned on you. Everybody will be so focused on Congress impeaching you that no one will care about FedEx being used to ship stuff around."

I closed my eyes to cover for the fact that I was rolling them. "If I just keep denying him and leaving no room for argument, he'll stop contacting us. The more excuses I give him for my denials, the longer he can hold out hope that if he just pushes the right button, he can convince me to give in. I'm toying with him. If I happen to make his superiors suspicious of him while I'm at it, so be it. Besides, Congress will be hard-pressed to prove I actually meant any of what I said to this guy."

"True enough," Sam agreed. "But if you run for election —"

"I won't be running for election."

He just looked at me for a half a moment. "You have a few months to decide before —"

"I'm not running. I already told the party chair what he could go do with himself. I'm not going to spend the next eighteen months pandering to a political party. I'm sick to death of playing political games. I'm not going to give it another eight years of my life. I'll fulfill my obligation, and then I'm done."

Sam nodded his head and changed the subject back to the matter at hand. "I wonder what kind of button he's trying to push with the package."

"He wants to see my reaction," I said, my mind flashing back to the conversation.

"Ma'am?"

"Let's send out a signal so he can watch me open it."

"You have no idea what is in that package. What if your reaction plays right into his hands?"

"What if I steel myself against whatever is in that box and just act happy or relieved no matter what I find? He hinted at a camaraderie when he offered to not give Dad back, if I pulled the military out. What if I keep playing the angle that I'd like to dupe the US just as much as he would?

"You're stalling."

"Yes, I am. I'm trying to buy us time to figure out a way to avoid nuclear war... Unless you'd like to just go ahead and have me level the country now. Of course, without anybody thinking we had proper provocation, other countries are likely to fire on us before we have a chance to go crazy and bomb anybody else we don't like."

Will got off the phone and shoved it back into his pocket. "They're looking for it. As soon as they find it, they'll scan it and get it down here, as long as it isn't explosive."

"Perfect."

"You wanted a conference call between the Speaker and the President Pro-Temp. When did you want to do that?" Will asked.

"You can actually handle that for me. I just wanted to update them and let them know it looks like North Korea. And that means we're looking at a nuclear war. Let them know that I've isolated two Secretaries, away from here, to preserve the line of succession in case DC gets obliterated."

"Are you letting them know because they're running the House and the Senate, or are you letting them know because they're the next two in the line?"

"Yes, to both. I need them to make plans on getting Congress together, if they haven't already. They need to understand the harsh reality that I may very well need them to declare war. They also need to be kept apprised of the situation in case our enemy succeeds in taking me out, or pushing me over the edge. But I also want to reassure them that if DC ends up getting nuked and everyone here dies, including them, that I'm taking steps to make sure the country keeps on running."

"All right. I'll slip into your office and do that now."

I nodded at him.

He stood and exited.

I went in search of another bottle of water.

"You should know," the Attorney General said, "House and Senate members have been quietly filtering back into town. They've all been careful not to bring any attention to themselves. They've also been careful not to come in on the same flights as others. It's been a slow migration. The families of the members who had remained in town have been slowly trickling out in case DC does get attacked."

"It's nice to know they have some sort of sense about them and have been quietly making their own preparations," I said.

It hit me again how the attackers picked the exact worst moment in our history to strike. This had to have been completely on purpose. No freaking way did it all just happen to play out this way. Too many things had lined up too perfectly, and none of it sat well with me. What kind of enemy sits around and waits for the perfect storm of opportunity? Let alone be ready to pounce, with this enormity, at a moment's notice.

Henry, and the original Secretary of Homeland Security, had completed the preliminary screenings and they'd come back clean. However, that didn't stop my instincts from screaming that something was going on with the two of them. Since dismissing them, I'd requested a more thorough investigation and a period of isolation for them both. They may not be my traitors, but they'd definitely had an agenda of their own. Whatever it was that they knew, and weren't sharing, was enough for me to order that they continue to be held for questioning and further observation.

I didn't know if I wanted the traitor to be someone my father had trusted so completely or not. I just knew I wanted the traitor. I couldn't do much about my dad, but I was going to get the damn, two-faced liar if it was the last thing I did.

By the time someone brought the FedEx package downstairs, Will was back in the room.

I took the small package from the FBI agent. "Ma'am, a word of warning?" the agent said. "It's... On the scan, it looked... Well, not pleasant, Ma'am."

I pursed my lips as I listened to him. "Thank you."

I turned and grabbed a pen from the table, and then took the box over to the desk and sat down.

The tech guy held up five fingers, counted down one by one, and pointed to me when the feed was live.

Since I didn't expect another exchange of words, I didn't wait for a response from him. I just began to move slowly, so he had time to sit and grab a snack for his show.

I placed the box on the desk and positioned it so I could use the point of the pen to slit through the tape.

Another slit, and another, before I could lift the cardboard flaps.

Inside was a large, felt-covered, jewelry box, the size of one for a necklace.

This just put my nerves on edge even more because I knew the jewelry box was meant to put me at ease. Yet I knew it had to be a deception.

I lifted the jewelry box out of the packaging and gritted my teeth.

I opened the box and inside, on a bed of bloodstained cotton, was the first two sections of my father's finger. They were the same two sections that I had witnessed the captor chopping off Dad's hand.

Dark spots swirled in my eyesight. In my bid to maintain control, I shoved my emotions aside and struggled to look at it from a practical standpoint before lifting my gaze to the camera.

This idiot had absolutely no idea what he'd just sent me. It made complete sense to me now. The whole idea of Dad pretending to be left-handed... it wasn't so that he could preserve his right hand.

It was so he could sacrifice his left.

The captor had probably taunted Dad with the threat of losing fingers before he ever started transmitting. I found myself shaking my head at the camera, a light of appreciation entering my bloodshot eyes. My Daddy should have trained for special ops, because the man was freaking brilliant — and totally on target as to how twisted in the head this guy really was.

I let the camera see my pride because I wanted my Daddy to know that I knew what he had done, that I was keeping up with him. I even smiled. For the benefit of the captor, I twisted some wayward piece of logic around to use as an explanation for my happy reaction. I didn't want the captor to know his captive had duped him and end up torturing Dad even more.

"This was the perfect gift to give me, thank you. I now have my father's remains. I can now offer something to the American people. I can have these cremated, have some filler ashes added, and make a big production of spreading them. You just solved a huge problem for me! I'm still not withdrawing any troops, but the amount of actions on your part I'll ignore before answering any phone calls from your target, begging for my help, just increased." I winked and motioned to cut the feed.

I put the box on the table. "Don't anybody touch it!" and I spun on the heel of my foot and went into my private bathroom in search of my contact bag.

I slid it from the edge of the counter to place it right in front of me. A flutter of excited trepidation rushed through me as I opened it up and started shuffling through the packets.

This bag had been the bane of my existence throughout both of Dad's campaigns.

Whenever there was a photo op or a televised event, somebody on the hair, makeup, and wardrobe opinion bandwagon was dissatisfied with my brown, puppy-dog eyes.

Funny, they'd always suited me just fine.

I'd been supplied with the full gauntlet of colored contacts. I could coordinate my eyes with just about any outfit they could put together for me. — Can I just say how utterly ridiculous the violet ones looked on me? — They still bugged me to break out the contacts whenever we had major events to attend.

Do you know what their favorite color for them to bug me to wear, for pictures featuring our father-daughter pairing, was? The color they had specially made, just for me. Why, it was my Daddy's particular shade of blue-gray. And the packets were plentiful because they'd had to buy the custom color in bulk.

I put the contacts in, zipped the bag back up, pulled my hair tie out and put it around my wrist, and went back out into the Situation Room.

I crossed the space to the table as I dug in my pocket to pull Dad's phone back out and held it up. "So," I started as I looked around the table, "are we ready?"

Those who noticed the eyes seemed surprised, yet doubtful.

Sam nodded.

I tapped the screen, slid the virtual button, and tapped in the password. The thumbprint screen came up and I didn't even try to hide my cringe as I reached into the jewelry box and gently lifted the grayish fingertip.

You could hear the uneasy catches in the breaths of the people watching.

I wanted to vomit again and swallowed against the urge, trying not to think about how cold and stiff the fingertip was.

It was disgusting, lighter than I thought it would be, and... unnatural.

But I talked myself into it because it was, after all, the same fingertip I had touched a million times before. The same fingertip had brushed my hair back in difficult conversations that I had tried to hide from, the same fingertip that had helped to embrace me when Dad had hugged me. It was a part of my father, and that wasn't disgusting.

I placed it against the screen and the print was accepted.

This was why Dad had lied about being left-handed. He gambled that the captor would mutilate the dominant hand. He gambled that the guy's mind was twisted enough, and I provoking enough, to drive the man to send body parts with which to torture me.

And do you know what that meant? It meant that there was something on the phone that Dad wanted me to find.

I gently laid the fingertip back in the box. "Somebody embalm these or whatever should be done with them. They'll probably be all the remains we'll have for the Presidential burial."

"We'll get it taken care of," Sam said, and held out his hand.

I gave him the box and looked down at the phone to see that the next screen had appeared, with the camera feature activated.

"You don't look enough like him. It's not going to work," Will whispered over my shoulder.

"You think I look like my mother's pictures?"

"I think you look like a mixture of the two. I can see them both in you, and that's the problem."

I nodded, "Okay. But you don't know what I know."

Will rocked back on his heels with a smile on his face and crossed his arms over his chest. He didn't know what I was about to do, he just knew he was about to be proven wrong and had decided to stand back and watch.

"I had an elementary school teacher who decided that a bunch of young kids could take on Shakespeare," I told them. "So, he made my whole class read Macbeth and perform it for the school and again for our parents. There were more boy parts in the play than we had boys, so a few girls had to play male parts. I played Banquo in the second act. Everyone who played a male part had to wear a fake beard and mustache for the parent's performance. What I saw in the mirror that night was downright frightening."

I reached up and separated the hair on the crown of my head. I used my fingers to comb it straight back and then holding it as flat and close to my scalp as I could, I secured it behind my head with my elastic band. — Dad's hair was very sparse on top. — I drew the hair over the sides and lower half of my face, covering it as a beard and mustache would.

I looked up and glanced around at the people surrounding me. Murmurs and gasps of surprise emerged. My chin and jaw looked like my Mom. The upper half of my face was all Dad.

I secured the hair across my face with one hand and held up the phone with the other.

If this didn't work, I'd break out the bobby pins to make the beard and mustache more convincing. I'd use some foundation powder to change the color of the top of my head. One way or another, I was getting into this damned phone.

I clicked the picture, the little circle thingy spun around as the phone processed the image, and then the main screen popped up with all the app icons in the background.

"I'm in," I announced.

I hit the texting app icon and had to search through the list to find the most recent ones he'd sent out, because he'd gotten numerous texts after the abduction that had gone unanswered.

"The Speaker's wife, he had been asking for an update on the Speaker's condition... Some standard stuff to some of the staffers, mostly senior staff..."

They remained quiet while I scanned.

"The Secretary of the Interior was sending him texts of tidbits of information on Rocky Mountain National Park."

"There it is," Sam said.

"Dad could have asked for info on the area in person, before they got in the cars... There's nothing about individual locations... Oh, my God!"

"What?" Sam asked.

I kept scanning, "Oh, my God."

"What?!"

"The texts between him and Charlotte are... flirty. Racy, even. There's a two-sided, mutual naughtiness going on here."

"Molly," Will whispered.

"I'm sorry, I'm stunned." I kept on scrolling... "Who's Felix?"

"Felix, who?"

"Just says Felix.... It reads like the person was on the trip with him. They discussed the possibility of a couple stops."

I pulled out my phone and dialed the number for the head of the Secret Service, then put it on speakerphone.

"Ma'am?" Ronald answered.

"Who's Felix?"

"From the Colorado trip?"

"Yes, who is he?"

"He was the driver of the second car in the motorcade."

"The driver of Dad's car?"

"Yes, Ma'am."

"He was texting with my father about potential sight-seeing stops."

"The driver of the lead car did tell us that he wasn't planning on making the stop, but that he saw Felix hit the turn signal, in his rear-view mirror, and begin to pull over, so he followed suit. When they stopped, the lead car driver radioed to the car behind him and Felix said the stop was on his itinerary. Which it was when we checked out the paperwork he had with him. We've been trying to find out who put the orders on there. The other drivers didn't have it listed."

"And where is Felix now?"

"He was one of the casualties."

"What about his phone?"

"The phone didn't have a record of any of the texts you're talking about. He must have wiped them out before he got out of the car. Since the papers had the orders on them, and the man was dead, we didn't dig further into his personal stuff. We will now though, we'll get clearance to dig through the text history associated with his number, then we'll find out if he could have had access to the scheduling system at any point immediately before the trip, to preemptively cover his tracks. If he didn't, we'll find out who did because they'd be in on it, too."

"I don't know if it makes a difference that the driver is dead."

"Sure it does, if he's our traitor, then at least we know that no additional information is being leaked. If the texts check out as suspect and we see that he had the opportunity to change the schedule for his copy, then we'll know to really dig hard to find out if he's it or not. The technology will show the crime, you just have to peel back enough layers to find it, which will be easier now that we have a specific direction to look in. The Department of Homeland Security has guys going blind reading through the text histories of people they thought might have enough access to information to be a part of this. The driver's text history wasn't a priority and they haven't gotten to it yet. They will now, though. I'll be in touch."

"Looking forward to it." I hung up.

"FBI and CIA are on it the case, too," Sam said. "Between all of the agencies, we'll get this guy pegged down and trace who he was talking with on the other side."

I nodded and handed Dad's phone over to Sam so he could have his tech guy remove the security features and go through the contents for any other necessary information.

22 THE END IS NIGH

I had to close my eyes and press my fingers against my eyelids. My head was pounding. "Does anyone need me for anything else right this minute?"

No one answered.

Will's hand clasped my arm. "Come on, let's get you horizontal."

I stood and made it halfway across the space to the office door before a knock sounded and the hall door opened. My nose took over my senses and my stomach rumbled. *Bacon wrapped hot dogs.*

When I turned, I saw there was freshly cut, ripe pineapple with plump seedless red grapes mixed together in a bowl. Something in my brain registered hunger.

And the sweet tea in the pitcher... *I was so parched.*

I went over to the cart and started filling a small plate and poured a tall glass, and carried them like treasures through the office and into the private study. And, once inside, I saw that some blessed soul had stacked my pillows and a couple of my softest, comfiest blankets on the arm of the couch.

I must have missed them when I'd come through to get the contacts, earlier. That thought reminded me that my eyes were bugging me. I rubbed again and headed for the bathroom to take the contacts out.

While I was in there, Will removed the cushions off the back of the couch, which widened the laying area. He unfolded the blankets and placed the pillows at one end.

When I came out, Will ushered me over to the couch, then picked up my plate and glass to hand them to me.

I scarfed the food down and chugged the tea. Just taking out the contact lenses and getting the food and drink into my system made me feel better. The glass and plate disappeared from my grasp as soon as I had them empty. Next thing I knew, Will was pushing on my shoulder to get me to lie

154

down.

He nudged me onto my side, facing the back of the couch, had me scoot in, and then he lay down behind me, spooning me. He draped the blankets over us both and reached over to the table to turn off the light.

I was exhausted. The dark blocked out the harsh and scary reality beyond the doors, and the warm body wrapped around me made me feel safe and secure. This was not at all my experience of the last couple of attempts at sleep.

Will's breathing had already evened out. I was gone seconds later.

It amazed me that when I'm in a crisis, the Earth seemed to stop spinning and time seemed to stand utterly still while I held my breath, waiting to see where all the cards would land. The sun still rose and set, and other's lives still continued on, but the people in the middle of the crisis feel frozen.

I think something inside of me must have unknotted itself, once it looked like we had found the traitor. For the first time, it seemed as though the Earth had started spinning again, and the clock began to legitimately move forward. Our future might be looking bleak, but at least we weren't groping around in complete darkness anymore.

Night had fallen by the time someone flipped the lights back on and started urgently calling for 'Ma'am' again, and again, and a-freaking-gain.

What was worse was that with the cracking open of my eyelids, came the remembering of my current predicament.

The people out there calling for 'Ma'am' were seeking guidance from someone who never wanted the job, never planned to keep it through the crisis, and was honestly just winging it out of sheer stubbornness.

I was lying through my teeth to the captor, creatively twisting the truth to the press, and faking a sense of calm competency in front of the staff. Of course, the competency facade had cracked when I'd collapsed... At least now after getting — I looked at my watch — a whole whopping hour and a half of sleep maybe I... *yeah, no.*

George entered the room after giving a warning knock and I stood straight up on the couch.

Will didn't move, just kept snoring. I couldn't blame him; he'd gotten less sleep than I had over the last couple of days.

"What's up?" I whispered.

He walked over and offered me a hand. "Everything, apparently."

I took hold of his hand and used it to keep my balance as I stepped over Will and down onto the floor.

George led me into the bathroom and put me in front of the mirror. "Try to do something with that hair while I shoo everyone out of the office."

I gave my reflection a weak laugh. I'd left it in my Daddy-impersonation state, in case they needed me to wake the phone back up for something, as they continued their investigation. I pulled out the hair tie, re-gathered it, and put it up in a bun. I grabbed a washcloth and scrubbed at my face, more to wake myself up than to make me look presentable.

"All right," I said upon entering the Sit Room for about the millionth time since this whole mess started. "What have you people got, to get this all wrapped up? We're coming up on the seventy-two-hour mark, here."

"We've got the location pinned down," Sam said.

I turned to him. "Don't toy with me. I'm a desperate woman."

He gestured up at the wall, where a map was onscreen. "This is the fifteen-mile radius that we defined earlier. Between the information that we've gotten out of our so-called Canadian friend, from the text log on record from the driver, and from hacking into the driver's personal computer, we were able to place them in an underground bunker about a mile and a half away from the military base."

"Why wouldn't they have secured him within the military base?"

"Because that would be the most obvious place to look. What we believe, is that they have a tunnel that runs from the base out to the bunker."

"Is there more than one way in?"

"There'd almost have to be. There has to be at least a ventilation shaft somewhere. That's what we're trying to locate now."

"Are we positive that spot marked on the dirt is where they're at?"

"Multiple scans of the area say that something is under there. Everything else we're finding supports it."

I turned my searching eyes to Sam's in silent question.

He shook his head. "The second they hear our guys coming, or see them bust through the door, someone is going to shoot him. A rescue isn't going to work."

"I know, but can we get his body out of there? Can we get his remains, to place in a coffin for the public Rotunda viewing? Can we lay him to rest on American soil?"

"We're going to try. It will mostly depend on how our team has to go in."

"What options have been proposed?"

"There're two sets of options. One for if the President is still alive, and one for if he isn't."

"And the options for if he isn't being more easily accomplished, I'm guessing."

"Yes. Tossing gas down a chute, and the like, adds more insurance that we won't lose any of our own people. But no American soldier is going to be directly responsible for the death of a President. They'll go in with guns blazing or something comparable, if he's still alive."

"And the minute they settle on a plan and I give the okay, I'm signing his death warrant."

"That's not quite how it is. The enemies are the ones pulling the trigger."

"Maybe, but that's not how it's going to feel."

"You can still sign yourself out. We can time it so you sign out just before they go in, so no one else has to know you've done it. The Speaker can give the final order to have it done, and then you can sign yourself back in. The Speaker could handle doing that much, even from his hospital bed. It'd be a paperwork nightmare, but it is possible."

I shook my head. "My father never once turned his back on me. I'm not going to turn my back on him just because the going gets tough."

"Then you're going to have to give the order."

"I know it. I'll get it into perspective. It's just a hard pill to swallow."

"He's sitting over there, with a throbbing hand, in mental and physical anguish," Sam reasoned.

"I know."

"The longer it takes us to get our plan together, the longer we prolong the inevitable. And the more opportunity they have to torture him further."

"I know."

"And the longer we wait, the less credibility we have with the American people."

I snorted. "We lost that the second we lost the President. Any credibility we might have left will be shot the minute it's announced that we didn't get him back alive. It's time we faced the fact that we're now viewed as being vulnerable by the entire world."

"I think nine-eleven did that, Ma'am."

"Not to this scale, it didn't." I scanned the room, trying to get a handle on what this night would likely bring. "I gotta tell you, I'd like to get proof he's in there and then take out the entire military base... and still get the body back."

"You'd spur a full-on war, if you did that."

I nodded. "Congress would have to declare war first. Then I'd just be following through on their decision."

"I'll start making calls to let them know it's time to assemble," Will said from behind me, announcing his presence. "But they're still going to want proof that the President is inside."

"Does their decision have an effect on your immediate plans?" Sam asked me.

"No. We'll still send men in defense of our missing President and leave the base intact until we can get the proof to Congress."

"Exactly how would you like to proceed?"

"I want to have our men in as close a position as we can covertly get them into, and then wait for contact... or we'll start streaming and I'll tell him I'm ready to discuss pulling the Navy back. I'll get him distracted, to give our guys as much time as I can buy."

"Won't your contacting him and talking about negotiation be a tipoff that you're stalling for time and maybe creating a distraction?" Will asked.

"Probably, but he's going to be suspicious no matter what I do or don't do. The question is how much does he actually buy into his own bravado. Remember, he claims I'm stupid and uncultured. Plus, I'm just a woman, after all."

"Okay. We need to get a team en route," Will said.

"They already are," Sam said. "She ordered that through text messages when she was getting the IV bags. They're on South Korean soil right now. They won't move onto enemy ground until they have her say so."

Will raised his eyebrows at me.

I raised mine back at him. "What? It's not as if we only have one team, and these guys weren't so horribly far away. When Sam told me it was an option, I told him to go for it and make preparations for them to go in. Before I give my final say so, we have to know if we're going in through an outer entrance, a ventilation shaft, or through a base tunnel. I don't want to have to have them hole up somewhere while we make up our minds."

"Agreed. Let's start praying now that it's not through a base tunnel," Sam said.

"Amen to that."

With the end of this immediate mess coming up, there was no way I was going to be able to go back to sleep while I waited for more intelligence to come in. I was going to be awake from now until the end.

Charlotte had been sending me e-mails throughout the day on a number of different matters. I decided now was as good a time as any to head into the office and start sending her some replies. There were so many meetings that the President and Chief of Staff should have been attending over the last three days, that the Senior Staff members were going bonkers trying to keep up with the ones that couldn't be postponed while we were two people down. Well, four down, if you counted mine, and Will's, current and former offices combined.

Two hours later, I was back in the Sit Room and we had a firm plan. But, like any other super-secret mission, hidden ten layers deep in classified information, we had to wait for the Earth to spin around and let night fall in North Korea. It was a long, endless night of waiting for all of us.

I just wanted it done. I wanted to be able to get out of this mired nightmare, know that Dad's soul had moved on, and start putting one foot in front of the other and move forward.

This whole thing was taking its toll on my entire team, as well as their departmental teams.

On the other hand, I really didn't feel like starting World War III, either.

Our hope was to go in undercover, clear out the underground chamber, get Dad's body, grab some computer equipment, and get out. Then we'd talk to Congress and plan our next move.

If we could sneak in and out, killing only those that are there, maybe we could keep the whole thing quiet. They would no longer have their ace in the hole. They wouldn't want it getting out to their allies that they had pulled off the ultimate kidnapping feat, only to be outsmarted and picked off by their victims.

Hell, with any luck we'd be able to use their own computer equipment to hack into their system and erase as much of their interactions and communications as possible.

Once we had our people out, I was going to order our nukes to be quietly re-aimed, and then slide our DEFCON rating to Two.

If the North Korean military moved a muscle, I was going to hop over Two and announce DEFCON One.

My very fervent prayer was that North Korea was not suicidal in their decision to try to take us out, and they would then back down without having the President to hold over us.

In the meantime, Sam had a team putting together information, and a presentation, for an emergency Congressional session that Congress was trying to keep under wraps.

On one hand, Congress wanted the people to know they were in the midst of doing something about the situation. On the other hand, we didn't want our enemy to know we were closing in on actually doing it.

It was still doubtful that Congress would agree to declare war, not until either we had irrefutable proof, or we had been fired upon by a known source.

And while all of us in the room understood that, it still pissed us off.

So, even though this was technically an offensive move, going in specifically to kill people who hadn't yet done any killing themselves that we could prove, we were titling this as a rescue mission. That would keep us on the side of defense and well within my official allowances. We were moving in defense of one of our own citizens, in this case the President.

However, since we wouldn't actually be getting the President back alive, it was doomed to be labeled as a botched attempt. And that was frustrating.

Here we were trying to prevent WWIII, and we knew going in that it would be labeled a failure because of how we were going to have to present it to the world if Congress didn't cooperate.

The poor Secretary of the Interior was aware of the plan. He had been informed that if DC should disappear, the backup set of launch codes were being held by one of the men glued to his side and they would automatically go into effect. He then, if he followed the plan, would launch whatever missiles the North Koreans hadn't taken out, and obliterate however much of the small country he deemed appropriate. As many missiles as possible were to be conserved to launch at anybody else who launched at us in retaliation for North Korea.

We were the United States of America. If we were going down, we'd be kicking and screaming the whole way.

23 WAIT... WHAT?!

As the wee hours of the morning wore on, George found out that the end of this standoff was coming. He very politely informed me that I was not to be on any of the upper floors, from here on out.

I wasn't even allowed to go in and attempt to address the press. With television being live and all, he didn't want people being able to figure out my exact location at any given time. He was worried about the off chance that someone might be gunning for me at that particular moment and would think they could somehow get to me if they just tried hard enough.

I'd holed up in a conference room across the hall from the Situation Room and took a couple quick meetings by phone, since I was not allowed to video chat for fear someone would recognize the room and know where I was sitting.

I spoke to the Canadian Prime Minister, and gained a measure more of cooperation with our ongoing investigation of how the President was smuggled through their country.

I then spoke at length with the Russian President, as I took him up on a previous offer of assistance. I don't think the man ever thought I'd actually call back and request his help.

I returned more e-mails. I brought Charlotte downstairs and went over a number of items with her face-to-face, and ignored my overwhelming desire to discuss some of the texts messages between her and Dad that I had read. I had Nikki come in and go over things that had been brought into the Vice-Presidential office because people didn't know if they should send those matters there, or upgrade them to follow me, since my old seat was now empty.

Everyone I talked to either alluded to, or said outright, that I wasn't being open enough with the American people, or the world.

What did they want me to tell them? The truth? No. The people didn't want to hear that we should probably be at DEFCON One, and that it looked like the smartest thing we could do for ourselves was to remove another country from existence. They didn't want to hear that maybe they should be gathering family and boarding planes bound for other countries. — Not that I could tell them what country to head to, because I didn't know how widespread this would get.

So, I kept my mouth shut. People didn't want to understand that if I told them all that was going on, the enemy would also know that we knew where they were. We couldn't very well surprise them if they knew we were coming. Why didn't I just go ahead and advertise all of our plans?

I got that they were growing increasingly frustrated the longer that this went on. No one understands that frustration better than the one at the helm, who'd only gotten seven friggin' hours of sleep over the last three nights. That's not to mention the rest of the team in the Sit Room, some of whom have probably gotten even less sleep than I had.

How about they just hold their freaking horses? We can't evacuate an entire country, all at once, especially not one of our size. Moreover, we couldn't risk the higher ups in our enemy's country having the opportunity to evacuate, either.

All I could promise was that, if we all died, I'd stand at the end of the line to the pearly gates or at the front of the line to Hell. But if I went ahead and publically declared that promise, I don't think it would set anyone's mind at ease.

"Madam President? We're ready."

I looked up from the paperwork I had laid out on the conference room table and saw one of the aides from the Sit Room.

"How ready?"

"Our guys are at the border, ready to cross. COMMs are all set. They've found the ventilation shaft and will be going in through it, once they get there. They're awaiting your order to go into the country."

I stood and started walking, one foot in front of the other.

I hit the Sit Room and all heads turned. My vision caught on the marine lit up by night vision in the scene that now illuminated the front wall. "Any surprises?"

"No, Ma'am," Sam replied.

"SEAL Team, can you read me?" I called out.

"Yes, Ma'am. I can also see you for visual identification."

Good to know. It allowed him to be certain that the order was indeed coming from me, and not someone attempting to speak on my behalf. "Wonderful. Are you the same SEAL that I spoke with earlier this week?"

"Yes, Ma'am, I am. Thank you for requesting my team."

"I read team's your files, and am confident I have the right people for the job."

Our deceased Secret Serviceman's brother smiled into the camera. "Yes, Ma'am."

"Are the preparations completed to your satisfaction?"

"We're good to go if you are, Ma'am."

"You understand what's on the line?"

"Yes, Ma'am. We've got this. Just give us the go-ahead."

I took a deep breath. Congress still hadn't declared anything yet, because they were still deliberating. I was teetering on the line between legal and illegal. "All right, SEAL Team, we are go."

"Roger that, Ma'am. SEAL Team out."

COMMs were cut as the team went dark.

"It'll take them about a half hour to get to the border. If their COMMs signal was just traced, we wanted to give them a pillow of distance so they could throw off anyone who might track them," Sam explained.

"So, we hurry up and wait."

"Yes, Ma'am."

"How long until we launch the entertainment?"

"Last ETA put us at twenty minutes."

"Is someone making popcorn?"

"Yes, Ma'am. The head chef said he's making chocolate-covered caramel popcorn, just for you."

"Awesome, will he make it in time?"

"He's on his way down now. As soon as he leaves, the sub-basement goes on complete lockdown."

I turned to Will, "I'm going to grab a quick shower. Nikki said she'd bring me down some fresh clothes this morning, I just never got to them."

"Yes, it took a Marine and Naval escort to get her to step foot in the residence again. They're on the counter. And you haven't eaten since yesterday, either."

"Nursemaid, much?"

"Rumors are you've at least drank enough fluids so far this morning."

"Shower first, then food while the betting pools start up."

He smiled.

I winked.

I was back fifteen minutes later. "Ma'am," Will said. "I just got a text from my aide. He said Congress won't declare war without proof that James Cartwright is on North Korean soil. They don't think you've provided enough evidence yet. But they will endorse any rescue or recovery efforts you may have in mind."

"Well, okay, we're all going to pretend I heard that *before* I gave the SEALs the order to go," I said.

"Ma'am, they're just about ready. Now would be a good time to place the call," Sam said.

I nodded to Will, who picked up the phone and dialed Charlotte to ask her to put in another call to the Russian President. A couple moments later, he handed the phone to me.

"Mr. President, it's good to speak with you again today," I greeted.

"Madam President, it's good that we can trust each other in uncertain times," he said carefully.

"I hear the concern in your voice. I promise our intentions are just as I've described them. I realize the risk you're taking in trusting me. I hope you realize the risk I'm taking in trusting that your military will not harm our equipment, or mistake our presence as an act of war, or that they will let out word about the true nature of the mission."

"My advisers are concerned that this might be an act of retaliation because it seems your President was moved through our skies."

"Sir, if my people couldn't keep track of our own leader in this case, how can I possibly be mad at you for not being able to keep his kidnappers out of your airspace?"

He sighed. "There are to be no weapons attached to any of them."

"I promise you, again, that there are no weapons on any of the pieces to be launched."

Sam gave me the thumbs up, indicating that preparations were complete.

"Mr. President, we're ready to go, if you'll give the final okay," I said.

"You have no idea what you're about to put the Russian citizens through."

"No, but I do know what this planet will go through if my teams are not successful. I also know what the American people are currently going through. You know what I'm trying to avoid. Please. I would not ask for your cooperation if I did not need it."

"All right. You have my permission to proceed with your plans."

"Thank you, Mr. President. I will make sure you stay updated. You should be receiving a secure link in the next few moments that will allow you to see our tracking of locations. You can compare them with your own monitoring to reassure your military that we are adhering to the agreement."

"You're welcome, Madam President. Despite our tense concerns, it is Russia's pleasure to assist the United States in this matter."

"Goodbye, Sir."

"Yes. Goodbye."

I hung up the phone and looked to Sam, "We are go."

He talked into his phone, "We are go. Initiate launch."

The dark screen from the SEAL Team's dead feed shrank and was lowered to the bottom left corner. The front wall now featured the current locations of twenty drones. All had spent the last several hours being quietly relocated to the furthest edge of Alaska's Aleutian Island Chain, to be as close to Russia as our borders would allow.

It was no secret that we had been piloting drones over the locations as we'd tracked the kidnappers' path through Canada and Alaska. We just never flew them back to their original homes.

"Mr. Favored Techno Geek?" I called out with a smile.

"My name is Alan, Ma'am," he answered.

"Alan, if you please, would you be so kind as to use our side wall to display the broadcasting of our favorite cable news networks."

"Only if I get first dibs on the betting pools, Ma'am."

I smiled. "You got it."

Like magic, they appeared.

"All right!" I announced in my best game show voice, because we were all bleary eyed and needed some livening up. "Time to play our own version of Russian Roulette. There shall be six pools. One for how long it takes until one of these networks picks up on the story. One for how long it takes for the press corps to smell blood and go ballistic. One for which news crew will start reporting with video from Russia first. One for which news channel will start reporting last. One to predict which news team will start reporting their theories as fact. And lastly, one on who is the first to actually guess our true purpose. Place your bets with Alan's aide."

Will's eyes sparkled even as he shook his head. "This really is in poor taste."

"Yeah, I know. But, we've been up for four days and we're getting a little punchy. Besides, we need something to keep us distracted while we wait. Otherwise, we're all going to start pacing and bumping into each other."

I turned and sat down to see a dish of assorted cut bell peppers next to a dish of almond butter. I started dipping. The popcorn could wait.

We munched, chatted, and laid bets as we monitored both situations. As odd as it might sound, despite the edge of the unknown future that lingered over our heads, we actually began to relax a little. We were finally doing something about the problem, and it felt good.

I still had the knot in my stomach, knowing that I had put into motion the events that were about to lead to my father's death. The only comfort I had was that by the end of this, he would no longer be in enemy hands. It was the only thing I could come up with that could begin to make it okay.

But then again, it was quite possible that I had put all of our deaths into motion. Maybe Dad and I wouldn't be separated for very long, after all. If facing my own mortality meant that I could see my mom and brother again, it might not be such a horrible thing.

I had to wonder if Dad was having the same thoughts, knowing that a move on our part had to be eminent by now.

Contestant number four was the first on the screen to have footage. They said it was video caught on a cell phone by a Russian civilian. They weren't yet willing to say where the drone had come from, just that the citizen had heard an odd noise and that the craft was flying oddly low, and looked too official to be anything less than military. The problem was, the citizen knew what Russian military drones looked like, and this wasn't one of them. People speculated that it was searching for something specific, and that is what caught the attention of the American-based network.

It wasn't the only drone people noticed. The pilots had been reporting that they could zoom in and see people on the ground checking different ones out as they flew past. The press just wasn't reporting it yet. Slowly, rumors began to build and a second channel switched to the mystery of the drones.

More pieces of video started coming in, from other Russian locations, of drones spotted in the night. As more stories popped up, more of the stations began to fall into play. The transition from the first station to the last took less than an hour from start to finish.

"Okay," I said. "Let's cut the public telecommunications between the US and Russia."

"Yes, Ma'am."

Chelsea sent a text within moments, 'They're circling the wagons.'

I smiled in response. The press corps was showing signs of life.

"All right. Let's cancel the flights."

The Secretary of Homeland Security smiled. "This is going to be an interesting phone conversation."

He picked up the phone and called the head of the FAA. He was going to tell him to cancel all flights to Russia, and to divert all incoming flights from Russia, in order to stop them from landing on US soil.

Moments after he hung up, a text came in from Chelsea, 'They smell blood. The sharks are circling. I'm thinking about hiding under my desk.'

"Mark the time for the press corps pool."

"Ma'am," the Secretary of State said. "The English Prime Minister is on the phone."

"Tell him it's a joint military exercise and that I'll send him a full briefing once it's complete."

He talked into the phone, then turned back to me. "He says he doesn't believe you."

"Tell him we're not bombing Russia tonight and that I'll explain as soon as I can."

"He says he's going to put the United Kingdom's military on alert."

"Tell him I said thank you, and to please remember who the UK's allies are, because they haven't changed."

"Ma'am, he's outright asking if Russia has James Cartwright."

"Tell him the Russian government is working with us. Tell him that we won't be asking him to choose a side between us and that I will call him back *later.*"

The news channels were going insane. You could hear the buzzing of voices in the backgrounds of the studios on air. Newscasters were having a hard time not showing shocked reactions as more information popped up on their Teleprompters. They were speculating that we were searching for the former President's location.

"We have contact!" Alan called out.

My smile was smug. The plan was working.

Alan cut all sound from the stations, shrunk the tracking map down and put it in the lower right corner of the screen, and then popped up the live feed from the captor.

He had the camera focused on another detached finger lying on top of a scratched desk. No doubt, he'd wanted to make me sick to my stomach all over again. It worked.

The Navy SEALs' screen flickered to life for about a second and a half and then went black again.

"They're on final approach to the ventilation shaft entrance," Sam said.

"A civilian in Russia took a pot-shot at one of the drones," one of the aides called out.

"Tell that pilot not to fly that low for that long. If he can't stick to the plan, as written, tell him to turn his controls over to one of the standby pilots," Sam replied.

I looked around the room, "Are we ready now?"

Sam looked around the room. "Yes, Ma'am. Silence from here on out. Anything you need to know we'll post in a box in the upper left corner of the main screen, so you can read it. Go ahead and see how long you can stall him for time and keep their attention."

I went over to the desk and sat. I gave a nod and a screen of our outgoing feed appeared in the top right corner.

"I'm a little busy," I said, talking to a finger, apparently.

"Well, yes, I can see that you are, Princess," a faceless voice said.

The camera tipped up to Dad on the left and an empty chair on the right.

Dad looked like hell. Eyes swollen and bloodshot, glazed with pain. Bruises and dried blood covered his face. His clothes were a wreck. Beard all tangled and matted. He looked like a man who had no fight left in him.

Yeah, it was past time we ended this. You're not going to suffer for much longer.... I promise.

The captor came onscreen and sat in the empty chair. "It's time you and I come to a final agreement, Princess."

The bottom left screen lit back up to show the SEAL's night vision feed. The top left read, 'Entering shaft.'

All I could do was keep him talking and focused on me. "And what is your proposal this time? I'm still not going to move the boats out. I've got plans of my own now."

He laughed. "I am not in Russia."

The SEALs were making progress, down a tunnel.

I smirked into the camera. "I don't particularly care where you are."

"You tracked the path of the plane to Russia, and now you have your drones looking for it. You think that if you can find it, you can find me."

"No, I don't."

"You won't find the plane."

"I don't have to find the plane." I slowed down my speech, as though I were teaching a lesson to a hardheaded person, "I just have to look like I've found the plane."

"And so, you're going to blame Russia?"

"Don't be silly, I'll blame a faction in Russia."

The wheels in his head started turning. "What does the Russian government have to say about your drones?"

"Are you kidding? They're so scared stiff that they're unknowingly harboring you that they're going to let us walk all over them. And when we do lay the blame on a group, they'll hand the poor fools over to us."

"You won't have your father, or his body."

"But I have remains, remember? He'll be a casualty, a sacrifice in the name of freedom. I'll make sure he gets all the military bells and whistles and services that such a sacrifice and title deserve. I'll just be presenting an urn instead of the traditional coffin."

"And if I go public with your father?"

The SEALs paused long enough to count off five fingers and then entered the first room.

"Look at him. He's about to keel over as it is. He's going to bleed out, or have a heart attack, or a stroke, or something," I taunted.

The enemies in the first room started dropping to the floor.

There was no noise on the captor's feed. I was guessing our boys had silencers attached... or the tunnel system was more sprawling than we thought.

"I can go public with recordings of your less than worthy plans," he threatened.

"One, I never mentioned any specific plans. And two, if you don't think I already have a team completing our own edited versions and re-recordings of my end of the conversations; you're stupider than you look. The American people and allies will believe my version of the story just based upon my history with them. You're a stranger who took their leader. I'm the one who's always been by their leader's side. They'll believe you're the one dishing up the edited versions."

He his teeth ground together.

"You've got *nothing*," I taunted.

"I have plenty," he hissed.

"You have nothing that matters."

The SEALs approached a door.

The screen up in the corner said, 'They hear voices.'

"I've been authorized to make an offer."

I sunk farther back in my chair and rolled my eyes with a broad smile. "This should be good. What is it you think you have that I could possibly want?"

"Cooperation."

"With what?"

"With your plans."

"You don't know all my plans, nor do I need your cooperation."

"We are a powerful ally to have. We could help each other."

"Really, and do you plan on telling me who 'we' is? Or are you going to continue wasting my time?"

"If I'm wasting your time —"

The SEALs were counting down on fingers, just outside a door.

"— then why do you keep bothering to talk to me? Do you think I do not know of your curiosity?" he asked, rather smugly.

"I think that if you were any real threat to me, you would have bragged about who your boss is by now." I stood and braced my arms on the desk and leaned forward. "I think you're weak. I think that pulling off one lousy mission doesn't mean much when you can't manage to back it up with a second or a third. That's what I think."

He stood up, yanked what was left of my father's left hand out, swung his knife up, and —

The SEALs flung the door wide and opened fire.

The captor on my big screen sunk to the floor with his eyes wide open.

Gunshots continued and three other baddies in the view of the SEAL cam either fell or slumped over. The SEALs kept their guns at the ready, but they ceased fire.

...And Dad was still alive.

Time froze. I stopped breathing. I was seeing, but I was struggling with the believing.

The captor and I had gotten loud and I hadn't even realized it. I guess subconsciously I was hoping that they'd know for sure it was mine, and the captor's, voices they were hearing before they entered and it would give them an edge. The idea that anybody else in the room could be so focused on the argument that they wouldn't hear anything outside of the room was a bonus. And, well, it looked like it had worked.

No one had shot Dad.

(Note from the author: 1/20/2018
If you wish to have your happy ending, I implore you to stop reading now. James Cartwright is alive, and Molly is the accidental hero. James can return, take a couple weeks to recover from his injuries, and then Molly can hand the reigns back over – with all the pomp, glitz, and glamor the United States can muster. Molly and Will can end the presidential term with a magical White House Wedding.

For over four years, the happy ending has been right here, all along, for readers to enjoy.

But, if you wish to continue, to read my intended ending, please do so. Readers either love or hate it, many leaving reviews based solely on what is about to occur in the story. From my perspective, I happen to love it.

Should you choose to continue, and burst the typical happy-ending bubble, you choose to do so at your own reading-peril.)

But... there was something... my eyes started scanning the room again. The SEALs all stood, waiting... for something. The view on both cameras held steady.

Finally, it hit me.

There was no blood on the victims.

No guts or gore splattered on the walls.

No bullet holes in their clothes.

My mind tried, really, really hard to come up with a reason.

The only thing that could explain it was that they had all been shot at with blanks. And the only reason to use blanks was if you never intended on harming anybody to begin with.

It meant the SEALs were on their side.

I closed my eyes, unwilling to look around the room.

How many of those standing around me were against me, too?

Were any of them on my side?

They were *so* going to blame me for the whole of it. They had enough sound bites recorded from my sessions with the captor to sink me in the hearts and minds of the entire population. The people would be duped and never know about the overthrowing of government that was about to go down in here.

Like an overwhelmed toddler, I kept my eyes closed and hid my face behind my hands, hoping I wouldn't have to deal with it, if I just didn't look.

I felt like how Dad had looked. Defeated, lifeless, just waiting for the end.

I had no idea if they were about to kill me, or were just merely setting me up to spend the rest of my life in a federal penitentiary. But right now, in this moment, I was the one who didn't have any more fight left to give. I was done.

Someone put their hands on my shoulders, and a familiar voice began whispering in my ear, "Molly..."

I was still frozen in place, trying to get a grip on myself, trying to figure out what the hell to do when I did open my eyes.

"Madam Vice President," Sam's voice boomed. "Congratulations!"

Soft applause erupted around me and I couldn't process what it was supposed to mean.

The hands on my shoulders squeezed a little tighter. "Molly, it's done, sweetheart," Will said.

Do they think I'm stupid? Do they think that I didn't see?

George's voice sounded, just a few feet away from me. "Ma'am?" and then a little louder, "Sir? Successful drill complete."

Silence.

I'd quit breathing again, and I was pretty sure my heart had just stopped.

"Thank you, George," my father's voice rang through the speakers. "Sam? Did your team get everything they needed to complete their portions of the drill?"

"Yes, Sir. Thank you," Sam replied.

Dread had turned to shock, and that shock had turned into a slow-moving sense of anger that was just beginning to wash over me.

My hands drifted down from my face.

"What?" I whispered.

"It was a drill, Ma'am," Sam answered.

My lip twitched.

Will let go of me and took three steps back.

"What?" I repeated a little more audibly.

"A drill, Madam Vice President," George said.

Through clenched teeth, and with a look that should have killed him, I said, "You specifically told me it wasn't a drill."

He took a cautious step back. "This wasn't a Secret Service drill. I didn't find out that it wasn't real until after we called the doctor in to treat you. It was then they told me, and I was instructed to call a halt to it if you were starting to cause yourself true and permanent harm," George said.

"Ma'am, this was a defense department drill ran by the Joint Chiefs. They wanted to test our readiness under extreme circumstances," Sam explained.

It took me the better part of a minute before I could find my voice again to respond. "Did the Speaker of the House really have a heart attack?" I asked.

"No," Sam answered.

"Did Frannie really die?" I asked, referring to the President Pro Tempore's wife.

"No."

"Was my swearing in legitimate?"

"You went through all the correct actions, but no. The cabinet invalidated the forms before the swearing in actually occurred.

"What about all the decisions I've been making as President?"

"I signed off on everything you did. You ran it like I would have," Dad said, drawing my attention.

"But I talked to foreign heads of state!" I yelled at up at him.

"Those we could trust were let in on the exercise. Those we were unsure of, well, you only think you talked to them. We had impersonators on the phone," Dad said.

"The drones, the news channels, the flights!?"

"That was real. People really do think I'm missing. There's a whole press conference plan we're going to see through, over the coming days. This was as much a test for the country as it was for the government. Plus, the news channels need to be informed as to how accurate their reports really were. And, for the record, Russia truly was on a joint military exercise with us... If you'll remember, that was a part of the decoy plan given to you directly from the Joint Chiefs, earlier today."

"Your hand?"

He held it up. "Whole and hearty. The fingers were fake. So was my blood. It was pretty awesome how they put my print on the tip they sent you."

All I could do was to stand there and stare at him for another moment before speaking again. My brain was having a hard time taking it all in. "Where the hell are you?!" I bellowed at him.

"In the basement of Buckingham Palace. I've been spending the week here in the castle as a guest of the queen."

I threw my hands up at my sides and took two steps back. "Oh, my God."

"I put the prime minister up to calling you and giving you a hard time right before the end all went down. It was my contribution to the cause."

Rage wasn't seething like I'd expected it to. "I can't... I have no words... I'm so... I... I don't even know what I am!"

"You are the Vice President of the United States, and a good one at that. You passed a drill that pitted you against unheard of odds, and yet you still managed to get me out alive. You just earned yourself a week off. Get out of DC, go somewhere and rest up, eat some food, get drunk."

I shook my head. "Why?"

"Because you deserve it."

"I mean, why leave?"

"I want you to have time to cool off and calm down before I get near you again."

"I'm not angry, I'm..."

"Distraught. You're in shock. The anger will come later. Now's a good time to get on a plane and get out of there. Especially before I give the first of what, I'm sure, will be many press conferences and interviews on this subject. Get while the getting's good. And then stay hidden."

All I could do was stare up at him. "Daddy... I..."

"You did an outstanding job, kid. I've got it from here."

I crossed my arms in front of myself. "I quit."

"No, you don't, because I don't accept your resignation. We'll talk after your trip."

CURRENT AND UPCOMING TITLES

Daughter of the Bering Sea (February, 2013)
Gift of the Bering Sea (May, 2013)
Bering Sea Retribution (October, 2016)
The Complete Bering Sea Trilogy (October, 2016)
~~~~~~~~~~

Lulling the Kidnapper (July, 2013)
~~~~~~~~~~

Looking to the West (December, 2013)
Rusty's Beautiful Skye (December, 2014)
Teddy's Drive-In (November, 2015)
Sweet on Coco (2018)
Luke Has Faith
~~~~~~~~~~

The Daddy Secret (August, 2014)
~~~~~~~~~~

Madam President (November, 2014)
~~~~~~~~~~

Walk of Shame (December, 2015)
~~~~~~~~~~

The Island Cottage (November, 2016)
~~~~~~~~~~

She Waves (September, 2017)
~~~~~~~~~~

I Used to Be (October, 2017)
~~~~~~~~~~

If It's the Last Thing I Do (December, 2017)

Find me on Facebook:
www.facebook.com/beringseatrilogy

174